LOVE IN PROVENCE

TRUE LOVE TRAVELS BOOK TWO

POPPY PENNINGTON-SMITH

Dear Annie,

I can't wait to see you again this summer.

When do you arrive? I have been helping your grandparents at the chateau and it is looking beautiful. They are hosting another wedding this weekend. I wish you could be here to see it.

Are your parents staying in France all summer too? Or just you and your brother?

Sebastian x

Dear Seb,

I can't wait either. England is dull and grey, and boarding school is lonely. Tommy doesn't really talk to me – I guess he's embarrassed of his little sister – and I don't seem to fit in with the other girls.

It's just going to be me and Tommy for the summer. We arrive at the end of June and stay until September. I hope you won't get sick of me!

Annie xx

Dear Annie,

I could never become sick of you. We've spent every summer together since we were ten years old, and I still miss you when you're gone.

Hurry-up June,

Sebastian xxx

P.S. I helped your grandfather to build a new porch swing this weekend. He says he will teach me to become a carpenter. I am very excited.

Dear Seb,

I hope you meant it when you said you'd never become sick of me, because I've decided I'm going to ask Mum and Dad if I can stay in France after the summer – permanently. There are great schools in Provence – I've already researched it – and it would be 'Tres Magnifique' for improving my French. Plus, we'd see each other all the time and I could help GiGi and Grandpa organise the weddings.

Say you're excited?

Your Annie xxxx

Dear Annie,

I am jumping for joy – is that the right expression? If you lived here, I would be the happiest French boy in the whole of France.

And if I learn to mend and build things like your grandfather... when we are old and married we can run our own chateau.

My dreams are coming true,

Yours even more, Sebastian xxxx

Dear Seb,

 That is the best idea I've ever heard. I am jumping for joy too!

 See you next week,

 Annie xxxx

Dear Annie,

Thank you for the most amazing summer I have ever had. Being with you every day was wonderful and I miss you terribly. But we can do it all over again when you return to LIVE HERE (!!!!) after Christmas.

I want to take you to the lavender fields, and go cycling, and to the beach, and to all the other places we didn't have a chance to visit yet. Next year, when I get my scooter, we will travel all over the South of France and do such wonderful things.

Your adoring boyfriend,

Sebastian xxxxxxxxxxxxxxx

Dear Annie,

I wonder if my last letter got lost? I hope not. I asked your grandfather to telephone you and check but he said you have been very busy.

He is helping me make something extra special for you as a gift.

Your love-sick boyfriend,
Sebastian xxxxxxxxxxxxxx

Dear Annie,

It has been two months since you left and I am becoming a little worried. You always write back, even when you're busy... but maybe I am just extra worried because I'm so excited to see you.

Perhaps I will break our letters-only rule and telephone you... or email!

Your Sebastian xx

Dear Annie,

It is Christmas Eve. I went to visit your grandparents to give them a gift and your grandmother was very sad to tell me that your parents won't allow you to move here.

I am so sad and so sorry. I hope you are alright. Do not be too upset – we will still have the summers. And when we are eighteen we can go anywhere together. Wherever you like.

Missing you,

Sebastian xx

Dear Annie,

It has been one year since you last wrote me a letter. I don't know why you stopped and I don't know why you're not coming back this summer, but I do know that I can't keep waiting and missing you and feeling so very sad.

Sebastian

CHAPTER 1

ANNIE

"*H*appy 30th Birthday, Annie!!"

As she entered through the large glass doors, the entire office erupted in a flurry of excited whoops and cheers. Annie pushed her sunglasses onto the top of her head and grinned. Beyond the huge shining windows of her sixteenth floor office, the early morning landscape of Central London glistened; it was going to be a good day.

She had back-to-back meetings lined up until six p.m. but Jeremy had booked *La Torlioni's* for dinner; the most exclusive restaurant in the city. He must have arranged it months ago. And Annie could only think of one reason he'd go to so much trouble.

Last year, their friends Chris and Emma had got engaged. Jeremy had laughed about it because Chris had proposed in his pyjamas after a rather heavy night of drinking, and Annie vividly remembered Jeremy saying that if *he* were ever to propose to someone it would be spectacular – not something flippant or spur of the moment. Of course, Annie had coyly asked exactly what *kind* of spectacular and he'd replied, "Oh, you know, somewhere exclusive. Champagne, dinner, dancing... a night to remember."

So, Annie was pretty certain that this was going to be it. After two years of dating and more than their fair share of ups and downs – being both business partners and romantic partners wasn't easy – Annie was going to get her night to remember. In truth, she wasn't the kind of girl who'd spent her life dreaming of being proposed to. And the thought of Jeremy getting down on one knee and 'popping the question' didn't fill her stomach with butterflies. But for the two of them to get married seemed... logical. And, as her mother frequently reminded her, time was ticking on; if she wanted to start a family, she really shouldn't leave it too much longer.

So, after fidgeting her way through the last meeting of the day, at precisely two minutes past six she grabbed her birthday balloons and her briefcase and hurried home to change into something worthy of *La Torlioni's* grand dining room.

She chose a figure-fitting black dress. She curled her long blonde hair so that it looked fuller and wavier than usual, she neatly applied the kind of makeup she knew Jeremy liked – bright red lipstick and porcelain cheeks – and squeezed her feet into a pair of far-too-high black shoes. Then she called downstairs and asked the doorman to order her a cab.

Her apartment was part of a small complex near Borough Market. There was a communal gym, a swimming pool and a sauna, as well as twenty-four-hour security and a stunning rooftop garden.

Annie's apartment was on the third floor and looked towards the entrance of the market. On a Saturday morning, one of her favourite activities was to watch the comings and goings below – people meeting friends, buying coffee, croissants, flowers, and fresh juice. It reminded her of the markets in France, where –

growing up – she'd spent most of her summers. Several times since they'd begun dating, she'd tried to persuade Jeremy to return with her and visit her grandmother. But he'd insisted that the agency was too busy and, for some reason, she had always ended up agreeing with him.

The PR agency that Jeremy and Annie co-owned was large, sleek, had extremely high-profile clients, and paid each of them a ridiculously high salary. But, despite the fact that they had built the business side-by-side, from the ground up, lately Annie was developing the increasingly uneasy sensation that something was changing. She just couldn't quite figure out what.

She and Jeremy had begun as friends. Straight out of university, they had interned at one of London's most prestigious PR firms and, after working their way up to management level, had branched out on their own just four years ago.

At the firm's two-year anniversary party, they had kissed. And after the kiss they had fallen into the kind of relationship that wasn't amazing and wasn't terrible – it just *was*.

Perhaps because they were too busy to meet other people, perhaps because they knew each other so well that it just felt easy or sensible... whatever the reason, they became a couple. And now they were 'Annie and Jeremy' – the power duo that everyone looked up to.

Except, recently, Annie felt as if the power between them was beginning to shift.

Within the agency, she had always been the driving force, the one with the creativity and the vision to see how big they could be, while Jeremy had simply been happy to come along for the ride. And yet, newer staff – the recruits who began as admin assistants or receptionists – seemed to be under the impression that Annie worked *for* Jeremy and, even worse, that she had somehow only secured her position because they were dating.

For a long time, she had shrugged it off. But now it was starting to irritate her.

Standing in the marble-tiled lobby of her apartment building, waiting for her cab, she tried to push thoughts of the agency from her mind and focus on tonight. Briefly, she wondered whether Jeremy would have bought her a ring or whether they'd go ring shopping together. But then she tried to stop thinking about it, because it was making her stomach feel woozy.

Jeremy was waiting for her at the top of *La Torlionis'* front steps. He was wearing the same suit he'd been in all day at the office and, momentarily, Annie frowned at it. Then, tutting at herself, she reasoned that he'd probably been stuck in meetings and hadn't had the chance to change.

As she reached up to kiss him on the cheek, Jeremy stiffly put his hand on her waist and pulled away. "Shall we?"

At a table by the window, tucked privately in the corner of the splendid dining room, Jeremy ordered them a bottle of champagne and, finally, smiled.

"You look lovely, Annie. Happy Birthday."

"Thank you." She clinked her glass against his and took a sip. She'd never particularly liked champagne, but Jeremy would be quite happy to finish most of the bottle. Looking around, she shook her head and tucked a curl behind her ear. "I can't believe you got us a table here. How long ago did you book?"

"Oh, before Christmas I think."

Annie smiled. Jeremy had never been very good at surprising her or showing her how he felt, but the fact he'd been planning this for so long and hadn't breathed a word made her feel like maybe finally they were heading in the right direction.

"Did you talk to Clint today? About the Bryant account?"

Annie flinched. She'd hoped that just for one evening, this evening in particular, they might avoid talking about work.

"Yes. I did. The notes are in your inbox."

"Great. And have you thought any more about it?"

Annie shrugged, trying to think of a way to divert the conversation. Six months ago, their old employers – the firm they'd left to start their own agency – had approached them and asked whether they would consider a merger. They were suggesting ridiculously large sums of money, and Jeremy was *very* keen. But Annie wasn't.

"Jeremy, maybe we can talk about something else?" She smiled, reaching for his hand across the table. "Leave work at work?"

Jeremy briefly squeezed her hand but then drummed his fingers on the crisp white table cloth. Nodding, he turned to wave at a waiter. "Let's order. Shall we?"

By the time dessert arrived, Annie was beginning to think she'd been wrong about Jeremy's reasons for organising such an extravagant meal. He had been distracted all evening, had checked his phone at least ten times, and had even excused himself to make a phone call mid-way through their main course.

Momentarily, she thought that perhaps this was all part of his plan; perhaps a string quartet was about to burst out and serenade her or perhaps a harpist would appear, strumming her favourite song. But as she scraped the last morsel of raspberry sugar crystals from her plate and marvelled at the fact she was, somehow, hungrier than when they'd arrived, she realised that time was almost up. The end of the evening had arrived and Jeremy had not asked her to marry him.

Annie bit the corner of her lip and put her spoon down, trying to work out whether she was relieved or disappointed.

"Did you enjoy the food?" Jeremy tweaked his eyebrows at her plate.

"It was wonderful. Thank you."

"Don't mention it." Jeremy had always had a remarkably formal way of speaking. Some would say 'wooden' almost. But tonight he seemed even more rigid than normal.

"Well, I suppose we should..." Annie trailed off, glancing towards the waiter as if it was time to ask for the bill.

"Actually, Annie. There's something important I need to talk to you about..." Jeremy briefly met her eyes, then looked down at his neatly manicured fingernails.

"Yes?" Her stomach lurched as if she was on a rollercoaster and she steadied herself by gripping the sides of her chair with her fingertips.

"I'm sure you've noticed, Annie... it's been happening for a while..." He paused and scraped his fingers through his hair. "Gosh, this is difficult."

Annie swallowed forcefully and felt her lips purse into a worried grimace. Jeremy did not look like someone who was about to propose marriage. He looked like someone who was about to...

"Things between us have been changing, haven't they? In the beginning, we both wanted the same thing but now I feel like we're both in very different places. And I think you feel it too."

Annie sat back, tucking her hands into her lap and trying to keep her expression neutral. "Different places?" She managed to speak, but her voice was shaky.

Jeremy nodded. "Exactly. This all began as a bit of fun, didn't it? And, well, I don't think it would be fair of me, Annie, to keep it going when it's clear that you're ready for more than that. You're ready to settle down. You want..." he waved his hands as if it would help the words materialise. "A husband, kids, a fancy house."

Annie flinched. She'd never really cared about fancy things. She went along with the glitz and glamour of the agency because that's what it was all about but, deep down, she could take it or leave it. He was right about one thing though – she did want children. Not necessarily right now, but someday not too far away. And she'd always assumed that Jeremy felt the same.

"But I don't want that. I'm just not ready, Annie. I want to be fair to you. And fair to the business. If we carry on like this, things could get messy and we've worked too hard to let that happen."

If he said 'fair' one more time, she might get up and throw what was left of her champagne over him. Suddenly, the sinking feeling in her stomach turned to something grittier and more resolved. Annie slowly licked her lower lip.

"Just so I'm clear, Jeremy – you brought me to the most expensive restaurant in London to tell me that you're breaking up with me? On my birthday? My *thirtieth* birthday?" She almost laughed.

Jeremy blushed and blinked three times in quick succession. "Well, I made the reservation quite a while ago."

"Before Christmas."

"Right."

"But since then your feelings have changed?"

Jeremy ran his index finger under the collar of his shirt. His neck was turning pink and blotchy. He closed his eyes, sighed through his nose, then opened them and quickly – like he was ripping off a bandaid – said, "I've been feeling this way for a long time, Annie. But circumstances haven't been right, have they? You were very, very low after your grandfather's death last year. And then the merger came up and..."

Annie sucked in her cheeks. She was trying to stop herself from shouting in front of a room full of people, which was no doubt the exact reason Jeremy had chosen to make his announcement in a Michelin-starred restaurant instead of at her apartment. "My grandfather died *eighteen* months ago, Jeremy. You and I have only been dating for two years... so you're telling me you've wanted to break up with me all that time? And, what? You didn't do it because you were hoping to win me round and force me to go through with the merger?"

Jeremy looked away.

"Is that it, Jeremy?!" Annie's voice was far too loud, and people were looking at them, but she didn't care.

Jeremy placed his hands, palm-down, on the table and spoke very slowly. "Annie, I care for you. Maybe I hoped that my feelings would catch up with yours. I don't know. But you've got to admit it's a complicated situation. The last thing I wanted was for the agency to suffer because we had a bitter breakup. But I just can't keep on pretending. It's not..."

"Fair?" Annie raised both of her eyebrows and folded her arms in front of her chest.

"Well, yes."

Shaking her head, she pushed her chair back from the table and began to stand up. "You know what, Jeremy. If you had just told me the truth from the beginning, it wouldn't have been bitter at all. We could have gone back to being friends and business partners, and everything would have carried on as it was before. But now? The way you've played this? We've got no chance." Starting to walk away, she turned back and loudly added, "I should have known what kind of man you were when you persuaded me that the agency would go under if I took time off to go to my grandfather's funeral. In fact, I should be thanking you right now Jeremy because, clearly, I've just had a very narrow escape."

CHAPTER 2

ANNIE

TWO WEEKS LATER

*T*he flight from London had been almost empty and when Annie stepped out into the bright mid-day sunshine she felt as if she might have the whole of Southern France to herself. The airport was unlike any other that she'd visited, and it hadn't changed a bit over the years; it was small and square with just one low-ceilinged hall for both arrivals and departures. There was a not-always-open coffee bar and no taxi rank. You could rent a car, but Annie had never driven on the 'wrong' side of the road before, so her grandmother had promised to send someone to collect her.

The last time Annie visited her grandparents' chateau in Provence, she had been sixteen years old. She shuddered at the memory and pushed it quickly away, feeling both guilty and sad that it had taken her so long to return. She hadn't even made it back for her grandfather's funeral. Thanks to Jeremy, she'd felt like taking time off would be damaging for the business. Even just a few days. Her brother Tommy, who was serving in the

Royal Air Force, hadn't been able to either. So, Annie's parents and her Aunt Susan had made the trip on their own.

On their return, they had shocked everyone with the news that they'd brought Grandpa's ashes home with them. Annie couldn't imagine her grandmother wanting that to happen but, apparently, Mum and Aunt Susan had insisted that Grandpa return to 'the soil he was born on'. And GiGi had given in.

GiGi was the name Annie had always called her grandmother by, because when she was little she couldn't get her tongue around the French word 'Grand-maman'. And, even as she grew, the nickname had stayed.

Annie hadn't told GiGi about Jeremy. When she'd called and asked whether she might be able to visit the chateau for a few weeks, her grandmother had been so excited – and had sounded so grateful – that Annie couldn't bring herself to reveal the real reason for her sudden escape to Provence; to put some distance between herself and Jeremy, and the agency, and the ruins of her former life.

Almost immediately after their breakup, things had started to fall apart. Annie had tried to carry on as normal, but then someone told her that Jeremy had asked Cassandra from Accounts out for lunch. A few days later, she'd seen him deliver a bunch of roses to Cassandra's desk. And after that, she couldn't stand it anymore.

That very same evening, she'd called a friend of hers who worked in private Real Estate and asked how much her apartment would fetch if she sub-let it. As it turned out, her friend knew of someone who was urgently looking for a place in Central London. So, the deal was done. Annie emailed Jeremy and told him she would be taking some long-overdue vacation time and that she didn't know when or *if* she would return, then called her grandmother and booked her flight to France.

Just like that. Her entire life had changed.

And she had no idea what she was going to do next.

Annie had been waiting outside the airport for almost an hour when she decided to give up, go inside to the rental desk, and beg for help. She'd tried calling the chateau but there was no answer and she had no idea who GiGi was sending to collect her.

Puffing her hair from her face, and marvelling at how it could possibly be so hot at just nine in the morning, she was about to drag her suitcase back inside when a white pick-up-truck pulled up in the space that used to be the bus stop.

Annie frowned at it through her sunglasses, trying to make out who was inside.

Then, slowly, the driver's door opened and a guy with broad shoulders and thick sandy hair unfolded himself from behind the steering wheel. Turning towards her, he waved.

Annie felt her mouth drop ever-so-slightly open. She wanted to say something but her throat was suddenly so tight she couldn't get any words out.

"Good morning, Annie."

"Sebastian?" If she hadn't been holding on to the handle of her suitcase, she might have actually weakened at the knees.

"*Bonjour*, Annie." His voice was like silk, or treacle, or honey... his French accent rolling off his tongue and bringing back floods of memories. Good memories. Wonderful memories.

Annie smoothed her travel-weary red dress and tried to slow down the tsunami of thoughts tumbling through her mind. She had no idea Sebastian still lived here. GiGi hadn't mentioned him for such a long time that Annie assumed he'd moved away.

When she booked her flight back to Provence, she thought about him. Of course she did. But she didn't think he'd be here, in front of her, all grown up and tall and handsome.

"GiGi sent you?" Finally, she managed to speak.

"She did." Sebastian walked slowly around the front of the truck and stopped in front of her. Smoothly, he slid his arm around her waist and air-kissed her cheeks one, two, three times.

When he pulled away, Annie was blushing furiously.

"You forgot that we greet our friends this way?" Sebastian tilted his head to the side and smiled at her.

Annie tried to compose herself. Three cheek-kisses was the way people in Provence said hello to one another. It was completely ordinary. An everyday occurrence. And yet it had sent Annie's heart racing uncontrollably. "I had, actually," she laughed.

"Then you have definitely been away for too long." Sebastian reached for Annie's luggage and smiled, as if he wasn't fazed in the slightest by seeing her again after fifteen years apart. "Shall I?"

"Thank you."

"I'm sorry I'm late." He picked up her suitcase and hurled it, a little too roughly, into the back of the truck. It landed beside a collection of wood, nails, and toolboxes which indicated that Sebastian had fulfilled his dream of becoming a carpenter.

"Oh, it doesn't matter. It's nice to be in the fresh air."

Sebastian chuckled. "Nice now. By mid-day it will be too hot." He gestured to the truck. "Are you ready?"

He was talking to her as if they were friends, as if things were completely normal between them, as if Annie hadn't suddenly stopped replying to his letters and broken his heart all those years ago.

Her heart jittering in her chest, Annie slid into the passenger seat and tucked her hair behind her ear. She hadn't seen Sebastian since the summer she had become his girlfriend. Back then, they had been so very in love...

"Your grandmother is very excited for your visit. She hasn't stopped talking about it since you called."

Annie shifted uncomfortably in her seat and fastened her belt. Her bare legs felt sticky against the warm leather seat. "I'm excited to see her too. It's been too long."

Sebastian pulled out of his parking space and began to drive towards the highway. Annie thought he might say something about her being absent from her grandfather's funeral. But he didn't.

After a moment's silence, she finally allowed herself to look at Sebastian properly. He looked the same – slightly wavy hair, piercing blue eyes, sun-kissed skin, slim but muscular shoulders – except now there was more depth in his voice and the hint of stubble on his jaw.

As they pulled off the main road and onto a series of smaller ones that led through towns and villages, Sebastian glanced at her and smiled. "It is very good to see you."

"You too." She paused and picked at the hem of her dress, just below her knee. "Sebastian, I..." She felt like she should say something – like she should explain what had happened all those years ago. But before she could, Sebastian interrupted her.

"Annie..." He sighed, his face suddenly a little more serious. "You should be prepared for a big change at the chateau. Things are not the same as they were."

Annie frowned and took off her sunglasses. "Change?"

Sebastian chewed the corner of his lip. "Since your grandfather passed away, your grandmother has found things very hard. It's a big place. And organising the weddings and events... it's hard for one person."

Annie felt a knot form in the bottom of her stomach. She had been so wrapped up with her own business in London that she hadn't really even thought about how her grandmother was coping with running the chateau alone. For years, Annie's parents – and Aunt Susan – had tried to persuade GiGi and Grandpa to either sell up or hire an events company to help them. But they'd insisted they could manage on their own – they were a team, and always had been.

Sebastian reached over and put his hand on top of Annie's. He had always been tactile but, still, the sudden contact between his skin and hers made her blink. Sebastian smiled at her, as if he knew exactly what she was feeling, took his hand back, and lightened his tone. "But that's why it is such good news that you're here. Do you know how long you will stay?"

Annie reached forward and began to fiddle with the air conditioning vents. The sun was beating through the windshield and making her feel too hot and a little flustered. "I was thinking six weeks... maybe longer."

"The company will survive without you for that long?"

Annie shrugged and blushed. "I'm owed a lot of vacation time, so it'll have to."

If Sebastian thought there was something odd about the fact she wasn't able to take time off for her grandfather's funeral but could suddenly be away for six weeks – maybe longer – he didn't mention it. He just kept on driving. And they settled into the kind of comfortable silence that Annie had never really experienced with any other person... as if they were two old friends who saw each other all the time. Not childhood sweethearts who hadn't so much as written to one another for over a decade.

Glancing towards the materials in the back of the truck,

Annie changed the subject. Smiling, she said, "So, you did it? You became a carpenter?"

Sebastian looked at her quickly, then back at the road ahead. "I did. Your grandfather trained me, like he promised. He recommended me to a firm in Montpellier but last year I started working for myself. Now, I rent the old stable at the chateau as my workshop."

"That's fantastic, Seb." Without thinking, Annie had slipped into her old habit of calling him by his nickname.

Sebastian blinked and his smile faltered. But then he continued as if he hadn't noticed. "It works well. I help your grandmother when I can, with repairs and jobs, and she refers all of her rich friends to me." He laughed and his eyes twinkled.

"She has plenty of those."

"Ah, not as many as before. But enough." When Sebastian said 'ah', he shrugged his shoulders. And this tiny gesture, and the tone of his voice, took Annie right back to when she'd first met him.

She and her brother Tommy had spent pretty much every summer of their childhood in France, because when they weren't at boarding school their parents didn't know what to do with them.

The summer that Sebastian moved to town, Annie had just turned nine. She was awkward, a little up-tight, and anxious about almost everything. But Sebastian, a gangly French ten-year-old with boundless energy, had instantly become her friend. No questions asked. Sebastian had made everything seem easy. For him, nothing was impossible. Dreams weren't just dreams, they were possibilities. But Annie had never been quite as optimistic as he was.

During the summers they spent together, they were

inseparable. But now they were adults,, the differences between them seemed to be magnified ten-fold.

Sebastian sat in the driver's seat with one hand on the steering wheel and the other dangling casually out of the window of his truck. His white t-shirt was crinkled and work-worn, his jeans had holes in their knees and, even when he wasn't purposefully smiling, his mouth turned up at the corner as if he was thinking of something happy. After the way she'd behaved, any other person would have been awkward or frosty towards her, but he was still just... Seb.

Beside him, Annie felt stiff and tense. Suddenly, her sunglasses felt too expensive, her dress too formal, and her luggage too over-packed. In London, they were what people expected. Here, they seemed totally incongruous with her surroundings. And, although Sebastian didn't seem to be remembering the string of letters he'd sent her, Annie couldn't get them out of her head. She'd read them, of course she had. But how could she explain to him why she'd never replied?

"Annie? Are you alright?" Sebastian glanced sideways at her.

She had been staring out of the window and turned to smile at him. "Sorry. Just taking in the scenery. I forgot how beautiful it was."

"London is beautiful too, no?"

Annie almost laughed. "In a very different way, I suppose, yes."

"You're happy there?" Sebastian asked the question in a very off-the-cuff way, but to answer it properly would have required far more insight into her current situation than she was willing to give. So, she just shrugged and said, "Most of the time. It's nice to get away for a while though."

"Well, France is very happy to have you." Sebastian smiled

at her then waved ahead. "Ah, look. Here we are... *Chateau du Colline.*"

Ahead, the black iron gates of the Chateau on the Hill gently began to open and as they drove through, and she spotted its silhouette at the top of the steep tree-lined driveway, Annie felt her lips spread into a grin. Leaning forwards, she put her hands on the dashboard of the truck and released a whoosh of air from deep down in her lungs, feeling just the smallest ounce of tension start to evaporate from her body.

"Welcome home, Annie," said Sebastian.

CHAPTER 3

SEBASTIAN

When Sebastian pulled up outside the arrivals hall at the airport, he honestly didn't think he was going to be able to make himself get out of the truck. He had spent three-quarters of an hour parked up by the river in town, staring out at the water and trying to pluck up the courage to do what Angelique Brodier had asked him to do – collect her granddaughter Annie and bring her back to the chateau.

The last time Sebastian saw Annie, they were teenagers and she was his girlfriend. He had smothered her with kisses, waved her goodbye, and vowed to write to her every week until she returned. She had cried as she clung onto him. She had told him that even a few months was too long to wait. She had told him she'd miss him every minute and would write to him three times as often as he wrote to her.

And then he'd never heard from her again.

Glancing sideways from the driver's seat of his large white truck, Sebastian breathed in sharply and steadied himself with the steering wheel. There she was... tall, blonde, and beautiful. The same. But different, too.

He released his breath, whispered to himself, "You can do this Sebastian. Just be normal. Just be normal." And got out of the truck.

CHAPTER 4

ANNIE

*S*ebastian drove them slowly to the front of the chateau.

"It isn't working?" Annie frowned at the dry, waterless fountain as she stepped out of the truck.

Sebastian walked up beside her and wrinkled his brow at it. "It needs to be repaired, but I'm not sure your grandmother can afford to hire someone..."

Annie placed her hand on the rim of the fountain. She had spent hours playing in it as a child, splashing her toys in the water then, as she got older, sitting beside Sebastian while they let the spray dance on their bare legs.

She looked up at the large wooden doors at the front of the chateau. They needed painting, and so did the window frames and the porch swing. At first glance, her grandparents' home still looked splendid – grand and beautiful, standing proudly on its little hill above the town – but now she was up close, she could see that there were weeds creeping up though the gravel on the driveway and that the lavender, which was usually springing to life in the beds beneath the terrace, was grey instead of purple.

Usually, on arriving at the chateau, Annie would have been greeted by the subtle hubbub of staff coming and going – gardeners, handy-men, and decorators whose jobs were to keep the property looking pristine. But today, it was just her and Sebastian and the broken-down fountain.

"Shall we go inside?" Sebastian gestured to the front door. Above them, the sun was growing hotter and brighter as it neared mid-day, so Annie nodded.

"Yes. Please."

Annie expected her grandmother to be waiting eagerly inside, but the large wood-floored entrance hall was eerily quiet. Crossing it, she shuddered.

"Everything feels so... still," she whispered.

Beside her, Sebastian looked up at the ceiling and sighed a little. "Yes. Too quiet."

"Do you know where GiGi is?"

"Ah, maybe." Sebastian breathed in deeply and shouted, "Madame, it's Sebastian. I have your Annie with me."

From the back of the house, a voice Annie instantly recognised as her grandmother's called back, "Oh, Annie. Annie! Come here!"

Annie put her handbag down in the hall and hurried towards her grandmother's favourite room – a large rectangular sun room that ran the entire length of the back of the chateau and looked out onto its sprawling gardens. It had high glass ceilings and the last time Annie visited it had been filled with all kinds of beautiful exotic plants.

As she stepped inside, Annie breathed a sigh of relief. Her grandmother's trademark orchids were still there, along with leafy green house-plants, indoor ferns, and a small collection of bonsai trees.

Annie almost threw herself at her grandmother, who was standing watering-can-in-hand beside a silvery bamboo, but then she steadied herself and tried to be a little more gentle.

"Annie, let me look at you." GiGi placed her smooth palms on Annie's cheeks, kissed them three times, and looked up at her. "You are even more beautiful than the last time I saw you."

Annie felt tears spring to her eyes and tried to blink them away. Like a tidal wave, the realisation that Grandpa wasn't there, pottering about in another room, washed over her. "I'm so sorry I didn't..."

Gently, Annie's grandmother put a finger to Annie's lips and, in her delicate French accent, whispered, "Shhhh. You're here now. This is a happy time. Not a sad time."

After embracing for a long time, they finally pulled themselves apart and GiGi turned to Sebastian. Lingering in the doorway, he rubbed the back of his neck and looked down at his feet as if he was intruding on something private. But Annie's grandmother reached for his hand and dragged him into the room.

"Sebastian, you will stay for brunch, yes?"

"Oh, no, I won't interrupt. You two need some time together. Family time."

"Nonsense." GiGi tutted and tossed her long white hair over her shoulder. "You *are* family, Sebastian. And, besides, you are working for Madame Despart this afternoon. You will need fuel for your patience."

Sebastian laughed and grimaced, then said something in French that Annie didn't understand. In response, her grandmother laughed back and patted Sebastian's shoulder. The gesture made Annie bristle a little and she wasn't sure why;

45

perhaps it was because – in that moment – Sebastian seemed more like *family* than Annie did. Perhaps it was because the fact she didn't understand what had been said magnified how distanced she'd become from France and her grandparents since she was a teenager.

Had she really stayed away for fifteen years? Away from Provence, and her grandparents, and Sebastian?

She had. She knew she had. But, looking at the two of them, she suddenly couldn't think of a single good reason why.

Outside, on the terrace behind the sunroom, a wicker-based table and four wicker dining chairs were positioned under a large parasol. The rest of the terrace was already smouldering in the mid-morning heat. But in the shade of the parasol, the temperature was just right.

"You two sit down," GiGi instructed. "I'll fetch croissants and coffee."

"Let me help you," Annie offered, lingering beside the table.

"Absolutely not. You've had a long journey. Sit down and talk with Sebastian."

Annie opened her mouth to protest, but beside her Sebastian whispered, "Don't bother arguing. She is still a very stubborn lady."

GiGi waved her hand at him and made a *pfft* sound. "Away with you," she smiled. Then turned and ducked back inside.

Annie sat down and breathed out a long slow sigh.

"Is that a happy sigh or a melancholy sigh?" Sebastian was sitting next to her with his legs stretched out in front of him, crossed at the ankles.

"A little of both, I think. It's so good to be back. And GiGi looks so well. But..." She looked up at the chateau, then out towards the overgrown lawn. "The chateau looks tired."

Sebastian nodded. "Yes."

"Shall I talk to GiGi about it?" It felt strange to be asking Sebastian for advice about her own grandmother, but he saw her almost every day and Annie merely spoke to her on the phone a few times a month.

"Not just yet. Let her be happy to see you first, yes?"

Annie breathed in and tried to smile. "Yes. Yes, of course."

Sebastian paused, then looked at her sideways. His voice softened and his care-free aura changed to something a little more serious. "It's good to see you, Annie."

Annie blushed and shifted uncomfortably in her chair; the growing heat of the morning was making the wicker stick to the backs of her legs. "It's good to see you too," she said.

Sebastian smiled at her – the same warm, cheeky smile he'd always had – and for just a moment, just a flash of a moment, they were Annie and Seb again.

Her grandmother's voice, drifting out from the kitchen, disrupted them. "Here we are!" She emerged from inside carrying a large tray that looked far too heavy for her. Annie moved to stand up but Sebastian was already on his way, striding over and whisking the tray out of GiGi's hands.

"Angelique, please let me."

GiGi didn't protest, and even allowed Sebastian to pour the coffee.

In France, coffee with milk or cream was unusual. Back home in London, Annie couldn't stand drinking it black but as she looked hesitantly at her cup her grandmother said, "French coffee is so good you don't need milk or sugar. Trust me."

Annie sipped at it, and her grandmother was right; instantly she wanted more.

"So, Annie, tell us... what made you come for a visit so suddenly?"

Annie had forgotten that her grandmother had the knack of being surprisingly, and unashamedly, direct. She took another sip of coffee, not sure what to say. "I just wanted to see you... it's been too long."

"It has been a long time, and you're always welcome." GiGi reached out and patted Annie's hand. "But you know you can tell me if it is something more, don't you?"

Annie glanced at Sebastian, who was watching her over the rim of his coffee cup. "Of course. But there's nothing to tell." She tried to laugh light-heartedly, flicking her hair over her shoulder. "I just wanted to see you..." She paused, purposefully meeting her grandmother's eyes because she wanted her to know that she was being sincere as she said, "I should never have stayed away so long."

GiGi shook her head. "You have a busy life."

"Yes, but—"

"Did Sebastian tell you *his* news?" GiGi interrupted, beaming at Sebastian. "He's his own boss now. And he's doing fantastically well. He is an amazing carpenter, and he is *very* popular... especially among my female friends." GiGi winked at Sebastian and Annie expected him to blush, but instead he just tipped his head back and laughed – a loud guffawing laugh that caught her off guard.

The sound of it, and the surprise, made Annie laugh too. "Well, I always knew you'd do it, Sebastian."

"Become popular with the ladies?" He raised an eyebrow at her.

"Become a *carpenter*," she corrected him, smiling.

"Ah yes," he replied. "Speaking of my work... I should go." Slowly, he stood up from the table and glanced at his watch. "I know French time is a little flexible, but I have to fetch some supplies for this afternoon."

Despite the fact that when she'd decided to come to France, Annie had almost hoped she *wouldn't* see Sebastian – because she was worried it would be awkward or frosty between them – now that she was with him, the familiar sensation of just needing him to be close was starting to creep back into her skin and the thought of him leaving made her feel instantly uneasy.

Trying to sound as if she wasn't really all that bothered, she kept looking down at her coffee cup as she said, "Oh, well, will I... will *we* see you later?"

When she looked up, Sebastian was grinning at her. "I expect so, seeing as I live just over there..."

He was pointing to a cluster of trees just a little beyond the driveway – where a small shady wood enclosed a stream that flowed down to meet the river in the village.

Was Sebastian talking about the wood? Surely not? He must mean the village.

"Sebastian is converting the old stable," GiGi offered, waving her hand towards the spot where the building was nestled, invisible from their current vantage point, in the trees.

"I thought you were using it as a workshop?" Annie asked, squinting at the trees, even though she knew she wouldn't be able to see the stable from where they were sitting.

"What can I say? I live for my work. It seems sensible to have my house and my tools in the same place," Sebastian said, grabbing a croissant and taking a large bite. "*Au revoir*, Annie. See you later."

Annie opened her mouth, but no sound came out. Instead she just waved meekly and then, when Sebastian had trotted down the steps, crossed the lawn, and disappeared around the front of the house, she flopped back in her chair and shook her head at herself.

Beside her, GiGi laughed. "He still ties you in knots, doesn't he?"

Annie frowned as if her grandmother was way off-base. "Of course not. We're completely different people now. All that... it's in the past, isn't it?"

Her grandmother took a sip of coffee. "Is it?"

CHAPTER 5

SEBASTIAN

*A*t the front of the chateau, out of sight of Annie and her grandmother, Sebastian stopped and put his hands on his knees, bending over and taking a long slow breath.

Annie must have noticed how nervous he was – when he kissed her cheeks at the airport, he had been so clumsy he'd almost trodden on her toes – and yet she was behaving as if everything was completely normal.

Sebastian had expected her to be awkward or embarrassed, and he felt he knew her well enough to spot these things even if she was trying to hide them. But she was neither. While he was struggling to remember how to speak English, she was cool and unflappable, and absolutely stunning. Which was making things worse.

Had she completely forgotten what had happened between them? Or was it simply so long ago that she wasn't giving it a second thought?

Sebastian stood up and brushed his fingers through his hair, glancing back in the direction of the terrace. He had dreamed of Annie's return to Provence so many times. And now here she was, and he was managing to do *none* of the things he had always pictured himself doing. He wanted to come across as laid back, unflappable, confident. But beside Annie, with her bright red sun dress and knock-out smile, he felt scruffy and awkward. The way he always had as a kid.

Back then, he had won her over with his humour and spontaneity. Perhaps he could do the same again? Perhaps he could win her back?

Sebastian shook his head and forced himself to trot down the front steps and unlock the truck.

Annie had been back less than a few hours and, already, he could feel himself gravitating towards her in a way he hadn't ever experienced with anyone else.

He had even been tempted to call his afternoon client and cancel so that he could spend the afternoon with her. But he needed to be sensible.

This time, he needed to remember that Annie Mackintosh would be leaving at the end of the summer. Perhaps sooner.

This time, he wasn't going to let his heart get broken.

CHAPTER 6

ANNIE

*A*fter their brunch on the terrace, Annie's grandmother took her for a tour of the property.

"You'll notice that it's not the same as it was," she said quietly as they descended the steps towards the lawn.

Annie took her GiGi's arm and sighed. Deep down, the proactive, highly-organised part of her wanted to leap into action, look at the chateau's accounts, list the repairs that needed to be made, figure out how to increase bookings and hire back some of the staff that had clearly been let go. But, trying to remember Sebastian's advice, she simply smiled and said, "It's still the most beautiful place on Earth to me."

They walked around the grounds of the chateau for just under an hour. Around each corner, GiGi dolefully pointed out something else that needed fixing. The lawn was dry – the sprinklers that kept it fresh and green, even in the heat of the summer, long turned off – the swimming pool was empty, the secret pathways in the Italian garden were overgrown, and the paintwork on the windows and doors needed treating to a fresh coat.

As the sun climbed higher in the sky and the heat of the day started to beat down in full force, Annie suggested they go back inside.

The interior of the chateau had always been a welcome oasis of cool and shade. In the summer, unless they had guests, her grandparents had always kept the shutters closed during the day to ensure the rooms remained a bearable temperature at night. Except for the sun-room at the back, which was practically a sauna because of its glass walls and ceiling.

GiGi took them through to the lounge on the shady side of the house and daringly opened the shutters. "It shouldn't get too hot, the sun is at the back," she said, sitting down and letting out a tired sigh.

Annie sat down beside her and put her hand on her grandmother's knee. "GiGi, why didn't you tell us how difficult things were?"

GiGi shuffled in her chair and shook her head. "Because your mother and your aunt would have told me to sell up. And I kept thinking things would turn themselves around."

As gently as she could, Annie said, "Are there any weddings in the books?"

Her grandmother grimaced. "No. I stopped taking bookings last year."

"You stopped?" Annie tried to keep her voice calm and steady.

"I had to, Annie. Look at this place... it's not fit for a tea-party let alone a wedding." GiGi sighed and smoothed her skirt. "After your grandfather died, I let things get on top of me. We'd always managed things on our own. We had a bit of help – gardeners and handy-men – but mostly it was just us. I should have hired someone, but I suppose I just didn't want to let go.

And now, there are so many things to fix and no money to fix them with."

"If we reopened for bookings..."

"No one will book a wedding here, Annie. Not looking like this."

Annie breathed in through her nose and tried to slow her thoughts down; there had to be a solution.

"Annie, I'm glad you're here. So glad. Because..." GiGi paused and breathed out sharply, as if she was preparing herself to say something that Annie wouldn't want to hear. "I have decided to sell the chateau."

Annie blinked hard. She felt her mouth open and close but she couldn't make any words come out.

"I know it's a horrible idea. But I think the time has come..."

"But the chateau has been in your family for generations, GiGi. You can't just give up!" Annie felt tears springing to her eyes as she realised that if someone else owned the chateau, her childhood memories, and her grandmother's memories, would be gone.

"Annie..." GiGi spoke slowly, tentatively. "I promise you my love, that I am not giving up. I just don't see any other way."

"Okay," Annie said, sniffing. "Okay. Well, why don't you let me look at the figures? I'm good at this kind of thing, GiGi. If there's a solution, I'll find it." She smiled, hopefully.

Her grandmother smiled back, but it was a resigned sigh. "Alright, Annie. You can look. But–"

"Ah!" Annie said, imitating Sebastian and raising her hand. "Let's just wait and see what I find. Okay?"

"Okay. But, tomorrow, yes? Today I want to enjoy my granddaughter."

Annie smiled. "Okay, tomorrow it is."

After lunch, Annie and her grandmother spent the afternoon drinking iced tea and playing canasta on the terrace. But at three p.m., with the sun shining fiercely down on the top of their parasol, GiGi suggested they go inside for a siesta.

"Afternoon naps are highly underrated by the English," she said gently, taking Annie's arm as they went back inside.

"Unfortunately, we don't have the weather you do, so they're not really necessary," Annie replied, although after her early flight, a short late-afternoon sleep was extremely tempting.

At the top of the stairs, GiGi gestured towards Annie's old bedroom. "You can sleep in your old room or in one of the guest rooms. It's your choice, my dear."

Annie nodded and kissed her grandmother on the cheek. "See you later." Then she lingered in the middle of the hallway. GiGi's bedroom was the opposite side of the house – a separate quarter from where the guest rooms were – and Annie's childhood bedroom was in the middle of them.

First, she headed to the end of the hall, to the room she knew was the bridal suite. It had huge bay windows that looked out on the chateau's gardens, an ensuite with a deep stand alone bath tub, and a huge four-poster bed. The walls looked like they could use a touch of fresh paint, but apart from that it was still just as luxurious as she remembered.

Sighing, she flopped down onto the bed and wriggled her feet out of her sandals. She closed her eyes and tried not to think of estate agents and potential buyers descending on the chateau, or about the agency and what Jeremy was doing with it back in London, or about the way Sebastian's eyes twinkled when he smiled.

But it was no use; she couldn't make herself drift off.

So, she showered, changed, and padded back towards her old bedroom.

Pushing the door open, Annie could feel herself holding her breath. The shutters on the opposite side of the room were closed, so she gingerly crossed towards them.

They creaked as she tied them back against the outer wall and Annie paused for a moment, unsure whether she could make herself turn around.

When she did, the room was exactly as she remembered it – and it was as if she'd jumped back in time and was standing there, fifteen years ago.

Her double-bed, with its white flowery bedspread, that had made teenage-Annie feel so grown up, was in the centre of the room. She swallowed hard and tip-toed towards it. Slowly, she knelt down and reached underneath. Her fingers moved back and forth and, just as she thought she was out of luck, they stumbled upon something – a box.

Annie pulled the box out from under the bed and sat on the floor. It was made of walnut and was a dark smoky shade of brown. She traced her fingers over the letters on the lid:

ANNIE & SEBASTIAN'S MEMORY BOX

It was still there. Just where she'd left it.

Her fingers lingered above the clasp. She almost opened it. But then she stopped herself.

It felt strange to be doing it alone; Sebastian had made her the memory box for her fifteenth birthday and they had filled it together, with things they'd collected on their adventures in the woods and fields around the chateau, with little notes to one another, receipts from cafes, photographs...

Briefly, Annie pictured herself and Sebastian sitting outside with glasses of crisp white wine, watching the sunset, and opening the box together – reminiscing about their magical summers, smiling and laughing at what they found inside. But then she realised that reminiscing would lead to remembering – remembering that she left and never came back.

So, she put the box back where it came from.

Unable to nap, Annie decided she would attempt to make dinner for her grandmother. Back in London, she rarely cooked. She either ate in fancy restaurants with Jeremy or ordered take out from one of the hundreds of nearby restaurants.

Opening the kitchen cupboards, she tried to think back to what they ate for supper when she was a teenager. She remembered fresh bread, cheese, olives, salads bursting with fresh vegetables. But there was very little in her grandmother's fridge.

She was about to give up, when someone tapped on the door.

"Good afternoon. Raiding the fridge?" Sebastian was leaning against the doorframe. He had entered from the terrace and was covered in wood-dust.

Before she could stop them, Annie's lips spread into a broad, cheek-dimpling smile. "You're back early."

"I worked extra quick today," Sebastian replied.

Annie looked back at the fridge. "I was going to prepare some supper for GiGi but there's not much in the fridge."

Sebastian frowned at her. "Nonsense, I'm sure there's plenty. Let me go freshen myself and I will help you."

Annie smiled at his sometimes-awkward way of phrasing things. "Alright."

She waited for him on the sun-soaked terrace. Now that she

was in shorts and a white cotton top, as opposed to a long floaty dress with too much polyester in it, she felt a lot cooler. But she was still relieved when she spotted him jogging towards her from the trees.

He took the steps two at a time, then stopped in front of her. He was looking at her strangely and it made Annie blush. Old Sebastian would have wrapped his arms around her and smothered her with light, enthusiastic kisses on the cheek. That was part of what she'd loved about him – he was so open, so ready to show her affection, so unlike any other boy she'd met.

Remembering that they were not those people any more was proving harder than she'd expected. So, consciously, she took a step back and said, "Okay Chef Sebastian... lead the way."

Three hours later, as the heat of the day finally began to subside, Sebastian emerged from the kitchen onto the terrace with a large dish of home-made pasta, followed by fresh bread that he'd fetched from the village on his way home, and a leafy green salad. Annie had helped him chop ingredients, but then he'd shooed her out of his way and insisted that she relax because, after all, she was supposed to be on vacation.

"When did you learn to cook?" Annie said, impressed at what he'd managed to concoct.

"Your grandmother taught me a few tricks." Sebastian glanced towards the house. "Do you want to fetch her?"

"Sure."

After her afternoon siesta, GiGi had told them she had some phone calls to make and had been in her study ever since.

Approaching the study door, Annie tried to shift the

sensation that perhaps GiGi had been on the phone to estate agents, arranging the sale of the chateau.

But when she knocked, her grandmother cheerfully called for her to enter. "Annie, I'm so sorry. I have ignored you all afternoon."

"Don't be silly, Sebastian's been cooking and I've been very helpfully watching him." Annie glanced at her grandmother's desk. It was covered with sheets of handwritten notes and what seemed to be maps of the village. "But you look like you've been busy?"

GiGi rolled her eyes at her desk. "Oh, yes. Come, I'll explain as we eat."

As they sat down outside, GiGi sighed and looked up at the sky. The sun was setting and it was refreshingly less hot. "Ah, that's better."

"So...?" Annie said, helping herself to a large serving of pasta. "What have you been up to?"

"Well... I seem to have agreed to organise our very first village festival."

"A festival? For our village?" Sebastian raised an eyebrow and made an *I'm impressed* face. "I didn't think Saint-Sabran was important enough for a festival," he said, chuckling.

"Mayor Debois is my good friend. She has been feeling... embarrassed that all the other villages have such grand summer festivals. She wants Saint-Sabran to make its mark on the area too, despite us being very small."

"It's become something of a tradition," Sebastian added, looking at Annie. "Most villages now host either a week-long festival or some festival nights throughout the summer."

"What kind of festival?" Annie added some salad to her plate and started eating.

"Music, food, wine... a chance for local vendors to show off their produce and families to have a nice time."

"And you've offered to organise one?" Annie glanced at Sebastian. "GiGi, I know you've done weddings, but..."

"I know," she said, putting her hands up. "I don't know what I was thinking."

"It'll be fine," Sebastian said lightly. "We can help, can't we Annie?"

Hearing him refer to them as 'we' made Annie's stomach twitch excitedly. "Yes. Of course."

GiGi smiled, then leaned in towards her granddaughter and whispered, "He's such a darling boy, isn't he?"

"Yes," Annie replied. "Yes, he is."

CHAPTER 7

SEBASTIAN

Cooking with an audience didn't usually bother Sebastian. But cooking with Annie was a challenge.

As she leaned against the countertop, her skin glistening slightly with the sunscreen she'd applied, Sebastian's brain was working overtime trying to remember what ingredients he needed and trying *not* to remember the reason he'd learned to cook this dish in the first place.

Angelique had taught Sebastian to cook after Annie left for England after their very last summer together. He had wanted to learn something to impress her when she returned, and he had practised and practised for months.

Years later, it was still his go-to dish and it still reminded him of her whenever he cooked it. But when she asked where he had learned to cook, he shrugged it off. Perhaps he should have said, "I learned to cook for you." But he didn't.

After dinner, Sebastian cleared the dishes and was going to slip away quietly back to the stable. But Angelique had other ideas.

He could tell from the twinkle in her eyes that she wanted to leave the two of them alone. And when she loudly announced to Annie that she was tired and needed to retire for the night, then whispered in French to Sebastian, "Have a lovely evening," he was certain he noticed her wink at him.

With Angelique gone and the sun setting over the gardens, Sebastian nervously cleared his throat. His resolve was already weakening and, instead of making an excuse and retreating back home to the stable, he found himself asking Annie if she would like to take a walk.

Annie, with the sun in her eyes, squinted at him and raised her hand to shield her face from the glare. "A walk?"

Sebastian tipped his head towards the woods and the stream. "The gardens may be a little in need of some care, but the woods are still very beautiful."

"Alright," Annie said, already rising from her chair.

As she stood, Sebastian couldn't help looking at her legs. She had always had long, slender legs. Legs that made his heart beat just a little bit faster.

"Okay," he said, brightly. "After you, Madamoiselle."

***

Stepping into the woods, the temperature immediately dropped and Sebastian noticed Annie shiver. He *almost* put his arm around her. Still, after all these years, his desire to protect her and be close to her was instinctive – coming over him in waves without him doing anything to invite it.

Glancing at her quickly, so she didn't think he was staring, he was trying to figure out whether she was still *Annie* – whether London, and time, and all that had happened since they last saw one another had changed her.

When he first saw her in her red dress, at the airport, he

thought she seemed different. But now, stomping through the woods in shorts and a t-shirt, letting her hand drift through the tall grass and pausing to look at the bark on a nearby tree, she looked just as she always had – pensive, calm, and beautiful.

"So, what is it like in London?" The question was utterly unimaginative, but Sebastian asked it anyway because he didn't know where else to start.

Annie looked at him, then around them at the woods, and shrugged. "Busy. Stressful. Bright. Noisy."

"And your job? Your business? It is going well?"

Again, Annie shrugged. "It's successful, I guess." Then she shook her head and turned to him, smiling broadly in a way that caught him completely off-guard. "But, I want to hear about you."

Sebastian rubbed the back of his neck and shook his head. "Ah, there is nothing much to tell. I'm a carpenter. I live just over there in your grandparents' old stable." He swiped his hand down to pick at a long blade of grass and began to twirl it between his fingers. "That's it."

Annie made a *pfft* sound with her nostrils and laughed at him. "That can't be *it*," she said, raising her eyebrows.

Was she asking if he was seeing someone? Was she asking what life had been like the last fifteen years, without her?

"Trust me," he said, "Saint-Sabran is nowhere near as exciting as London. *I* don't get to meet celebrities like Maya Wallace and George Turner."

Annie stopped walking. She was frowning at him. "How did you know...?"

"I might have Googled you, once or twice..." Sebastian said the words before he had the chance to even think about them. And the second they left his lips, he felt his cheeks flush a furious shade of pink.

"You Googled me?" He couldn't tell whether she found it amusing or not.

"Just once... or twice."

"Well," said Annie. "I might have Googled you too."

CHAPTER 8

ANNIE

*A*nnie woke to the sound of a rooster crowing. She'd forgotten about the chickens her grandmother kept, and she'd forgotten how annoying the rooster was.

Usually, the shutters kept the bedrooms so dark that it was easy to sleep in way past the sun rising. But last night the heat and humidity had been almost unbearable, so Annie had opted to keep them open.

Her grandparents had installed air-conditioning several years ago, because the wedding guests wanted it, but the system was expensive to run and had been switched off for months. So, Annie had spent most of the night tossing and turning and slowly sweltering.

Had summers in Provence always been this hot? Or had they become more vicious since she'd last visited?

Downstairs, she made herself some coffee and took it outside. If the pool had been full, she might have gone for an early-morning swim or sat beside it and dangled her feet in, but instead she perched on the top step of the terrace, just in front of the sunroom, looking towards Sebastian's hidden house in the woods.

As if he'd sensed that she was there, not long after she sat down, Sebastian emerged from the trees and waved at her.

He was carrying his own flask of coffee.

"Morning," Annie said, smiling.

"Morning." Sebastian sat down and brushed his fingers through his thick floppy hair. He yawned and rubbed his eyes.

"Late night?" Annie asked. They'd finished their walk just before sunset and said goodnight on the terrace. By ten, Annie had been in bed and she'd assumed that Sebastian would have been too. But maybe he couldn't sleep either. Maybe the heat of the converted stable was too much. Or maybe he was wondering exactly how many times she had Googled him over the years – she really shouldn't have admitted to that.

"I was working on a project for far too many hours." Sebastian grinned sheepishly. "I think it was three a.m. when I went to bed."

"What were you working on?" Annie stretched her legs out in front of her and felt herself start to relax. It had always been this way with Sebastian, even after they spent a long time apart between summers – when she saw him, her heart did somersaults, but as soon as they started talking, she felt completely at ease.

Sebastian tapped the side of his nose with his index finger. "Top secret, I'm afraid."

Annie was about to press him to say more, perhaps nudge his side with her elbow and tease him a little, when a strange noise from inside the house interrupted their conversation.

"What was that?" she asked, glancing back towards the sunroom.

"I have no idea."

67

They walked slowly inside, half expecting to see that a bird had found its way in amongst the orchids and had knocked something over.

The sunroom was empty, except for its collection of exotic plants. But as Annie entered the chateau's grand entrance hall, she let out a short stifled scream. "GiGi?!"

Her grandmother was lying at the bottom of the stairs, and there was blood on the floor.

Immediately, Sebastian took out his cell phone and called an ambulance while Annie bent down and pushed the hair from her grandmother's face.

"GiGi? Can you hear me?"

GiGi opened her eyes and smiled a very weak smile. "I think I fell."

Relief washed over Annie. "Yes, I think you did."

As her grandmother tried to move, she winced and cried out.

"Stay still," Annie said. "Don't try to move until the ambulance gets here."

"Angelique? Can you tell us what hurts?" Sebastian knelt down beside Annie and her grandmother.

GiGi groaned. "Oh Sebastian, how embarrassing."

"Nonsense. I've taken a fall many times in my workshop..." He smiled and squeezed her hand.

"Everything hurts," she replied. "But I think my arm is the worst."

"Alright, don't worry, the ambulance will be here soon."

Four hours later, Annie and Sebastian found themselves sitting beside GiGi's hospital bed, smiling while she regaled the nurses with the full gory details of her fall.

She had broken her arm and had a cut on her head where she'd caught it on the banister, so the doctors wanted to keep her in for a couple of days' observation. They also wanted to run some tests so they could make sure the fall hadn't been due to anything more sinister than simply low blood sugar or feeling a little dizzy.

"Oh, I am a silly old woman," GiGi said for the fiftieth time.

"Accidents happen," Annie tutted. "Now, what would you like us to bring you from home?"

Annie's grandmother reeled off a long list of items, then suddenly seemed to come over extremely tired.

"Alright, Angelique. We will fetch your things and see you later." Sebastian patted her hand and stood up, gesturing to Annie that they should probably leave.

"Thank you," GiGi said, softly. Then just as Annie began to rise from her chair, she added. "Annie... the festival. Mayor Debois was expecting me to call her with some arrangements. Can you explain what has happened? I'm not sure I will be able to continue organising it. If I knew how long they'd want me to stay in here–"

"Of course," Annie said, patting her hand. "Don't worry about a thing. We'll sort it all out."

Back at the chateau, Annie burst into tears as soon as they crossed the threshold. Stepping towards her, Sebastian wrapped her in a large tight hug. "She's alright, Annie. She's going to be fine."

"But if we hadn't been here..." Annie pulled away from him, wiping at her tear-stained cheeks. "She shouldn't be living here alone."

"It's okay Annie," Sebastian put his large firm hands on her upper arms and gave a little squeeze. "I live just outside. I check on her every day."

"But you shouldn't be doing that Sebastian, she's not your grandmother..."

Sebastian blinked and slowly took back his hands. His expression had changed and Annie felt as if she'd upset him somehow. "No, she isn't. But she's the closest thing to family I have. She has always looked after me, so I look after her as best as I can."

Annie shook her head. "Of course you do. I didn't mean to make it sound as if..." She stopped and took a deep breath, letting the air fill her lungs and calm her down. "I'm sorry Sebastian. It's all just been a little overwhelming."

Sebastian sighed and, for the first time – possibly in the entire time she'd known him – his face crumpled into an expression that made him look deeply worried. "If you collect the things she asked for, I'll call the mayor and explain what has happened."

"Alright," Annie nodded and, as she walked towards the stairs, stopped and looked back. "Sebastian, what about your work? Surely you can't just take an entire day..."

"My client will understand, she is a friend of your grandmother."

Annie smiled at him, but she could see that she'd dented his feelings.

Sebastian's parents had died when he was just nine years old, which was why he'd moved to the village of Saint-Sabran – to live with his aunt. She had done her best, but she hadn't been particularly warm or loving towards him and Annie knew that Sebastian had always doted on her grandparents. She shouldn't have reminded him that they weren't his real family, and she wished furiously that she could take it back.

She opened her mouth to apologise, to try and make it better, but he was already walking away.

Annie had just finished packing her grandmother's clothes and toiletries into a quilted overnight bag when Sebastian tapped on the door.

"Come in, I'm almost finished," Annie called, folding a soft pink nightdress and squeezing it in beside a wash bag full of soap. As she waited for Sebastian to appear, she held her breath, praying he wasn't still feeling hurt by her thoughtlessness.

But when Sebastian's head popped around the door, he looked just as he always did. Handsome and smiling, he waved his phone at her. "I spoke with Mayor Debois."

"What did she say?" Annie zipped up the overnight bag and jostled it onto her shoulder.

"She would like to come and talk with you."

"Me?" Annie frowned. "Why?"

"She is very sad about your grandmother being hurt, of course, but also she is worried because so many people were excited about the festival." Sebastian paused and rubbed the back of his neck. "She is hoping that you might..."

For a moment, Annie couldn't figure out what Sebastian was saying, but then slowly it dawned on her. "She wants *me* to organise it?"

"Would you?" Sebastian asked, quietly, as if he didn't want to scare her.

"I..." Annie's head was swimming. A couple of days ago, she'd been in London, power-dressing and attending meetings with celebrity clients. Yesterday, her world had been thrown head-first into a whirlwind of emotion because of Sebastian and the chateau and GiGi's talk of selling-up. And now, her grandmother was in hospital and the mayor of Saint-Sabran was asking her to step in and organise a *festival*.

Annie swallowed forcefully. "We don't know how long GiGi will be in hospital for, Sebastian. She might be able to..." She trailed off. Sebastian was looking at her with his wide, sparkling blue eyes. Eyes that made it almost impossible to say no. "Let me think about it. I'll talk with Mayor Debois. Of course, I will."

"Great," Sebastian's lips spread into a knowing grin, clearly he was no longer upset with her. "I already told her you would – she's coming by this evening."

Annie put her hands on her hips and shook her head at him.

"Ah, I missed that look," he said, his eyes taking her in, making her feel nervous and shy and self-assured all at once.

"We should get going." Annie tutted and gestured to the door, trying not to smile at him.

"Yes," he said. "We should. Shall we go through the village? Pick up some flowers?"

"Of course," Annie nodded. "She'd love that."

Downstairs, they locked the large wooden front doors and headed towards the garage at the side of the house. Annie assumed they'd be taking Sebastian's truck, but when they got there he gestured to a small mint-green scooter and handed her a helmet.

Annie's eyes widened as she took it in. "Sebastian... you did it! You got your scooter!"

"I did," he replied, climbing on without bothering with a helmet for himself. "Quite a few years ago now. I use the truck, mostly. But the scooter is nice on a day like this." He looked up at the cloudless sky then patted the scooter's handlebars. "Want to drive?" he asked her, tilting his head playfully.

"Um, no." Annie fastened her helmet and climbed on behind him. "I'll leave that to the professional, thank you."

"Okay then, off we go..." Sebastian zoomed out of the driveway, down the tree-lined entrance to the property and through the large black gates that shielded them from the rest of the world.

The chateau stood on a hill – hence its name *Chateau du Colline*– and as they wound their way down towards the village, the breeze on Annie's face was overwhelmingly refreshing. She breathed deeply and tilted her face up at the sun; this was what she and Sebastian had always talked about. They had dreamed of buying a scooter and setting off on adventures together... discovering all of the wonders that the beautiful South of France had to offer.

Back then, Annie and Sebastian had been rather bored with Saint-Sabran. They had ambitions to travel further, to the lavender fields, and the picturesque cities, and the Pond du Gard – a giant Roman aqueduct that teenagers often jumped from into the river, despite the fact it was far too dangerous. And Annie had always longed to visit *Les Beaux du Provence* – a town carved into a rocky hillside, with spectacular views across the surrounding valleys.

On the plane ride over, she'd thought about all of those things. She'd thought about hiring a car and taking GiGi with her to do some sight-seeing. But now she was here, on the back of Sebastian's scooter, with her arms around his waist and the sun on her face, she didn't care where she was. She didn't care whether she was standing at the top of the Pond du Gard looking down at a wide sparkling river or simply riding through sleepy

Saint-Sabran with the sun on her face – she could think of
nowhere else she'd rather be.

As they approached the village, Annie peered over
Sebastian's shoulder and smiled. It felt good to be seeing it again.

Saint-Sabran was small but perfectly formed – surrounded
on three sides by a wide, slow moving river, it was accessed by
either bridges or a small one-car road. The buildings were
typical of the South of France – tall, light stone, with blue
shutters and Juliet balconies that housed colourful plants.

The centre of the village was made up of a collection of
shops and restaurants that opened onto a square with a fountain
in its middle, and this was where Sebastian stopped. Driving
under the archway of the clocktower that stood at the head of the
square, he pulled up beside the florist's and told Annie he'd be
right back.

A few moments later, he returned with a bouquet of
sunflowers and handed them to Annie.

She beamed at them. "These are my favourite."

"I know," Sebastian said, smiling coyly. "This is why they are
for you."

Annie looked up from sniffing them. Even though they
didn't give off a scent, she just loved to breathe them in. "Me?"

"Ah, yes." Sebastian was trying to seem nonchalant about it
but Annie was sure that he was blushing.

"What about GiGi?"

As she spoke, a short middle-aged woman with black hair
emerged from the florist's. She was holding a purple orchid and
said something to Annie in French as she handed it over.

"She says, 'Can you manage?'" Sebastian asked.

"Of course," Annie said to the florist, wishing she could
make her brain work quickly enough to translate the phrase into
French. "*Merci.*"

Handing Sebastian back the sunflowers, she asked him to strap them to the back of the scooter, along with GiGi's overnight bag, so that she could hold on to the orchid. "She will love it, Sebastian. Thank you."

Sebastian smiled, climbing back on in front of her. "No need to thank me."

Annie smiled and, with the orchid tucked under one arm, wrapped the other around Sebastian's waist. How many times had she dreamed of doing this when she was a teenager? How many times had she lain awake at night just wanting to be near him?

As they pulled out of the village square, Annie tightened her grip. At least for the next twenty minutes, she wasn't letting go.

CHAPTER 9

ANNIE

*A*t the hospital, GiGi informed Annie and Sebastian that her stay might be a little longer than they first anticipated; her doctors were worried that the fall had been caused by a dizzy spell, and that a dizzy spell could be a sign of something more serious.

After hearing this, Annie was reluctant to leave her grandmother but Sebastian took her hand and told her everything would be alright.

Still, when they returned to the chateau they were both a little more subdued than when they'd left it.

Walking through the house, Annie headed to the sunroom to water her grandmother's orchids. GiGi loved the one Sebastian had picked out for her and had asked the nurse to display it proudly on the reception desk outside so that everyone could enjoy it.

It was stiflingly hot in the sunroom. Outside, it was almost thirty-five degrees and the large glass windows seemed to magnify the heat. But, still, Annie sat for a moment on GiGi's little indoor bench and breathed in the smell that she remembered so well from her childhood – earth and moisture and greenness.

When Sebastian appeared with iced tea, they headed out to the terrace. "Shall we go down to the pool?" he asked. And, for a moment, Annie forgot that it was empty. She pictured dipping her feet into the water and letting it cool her toes.

"The pool?"

"It's shady down there, and there's often a little bit of a breeze. The terrace is a sun-trap at this time of day."

Annie nodded and followed him. Together, they sat on worn out wooden deck chairs beneath the shade of a large olive tree that Annie remembered her grandfather planting, looking at the waterless swimming pool.

"I'd give pretty much anything for a swim right now," Annie said wistfully, resting her sunglasses on her nose and wondering whether she should have added another layer of sunscreen, despite the fact they weren't in direct sunlight.

"Perhaps tomorrow we could go to the Lido?" Sebastian glanced at her quickly as he asked the question, as if she might say no.

"That would be great. Are you working tomorrow?"

Sebastian laughed and stretched out his legs. "Tomorrow is a bank holiday."

Annie frowned. In London, especially in her business, public holidays meant very little. She worked evenings, weekends, holidays... in fact before coming back to Saint-Sabran she hadn't had a day off – apart from Christmas Day – since they'd started the business.

"In France, no one works bank holidays," Sebastian said with a smile. "In fact, maybe we could go to the coast? The beach will be busy but if we leave early..."

Annie hesitated and felt her nose wrinkle.

Sebastian, reading it as a sign she wasn't keen, shook his head and looked down into his iced tea. "It doesn't matter... just an idea."

"No, I'd love to," Annie said, dipping her head so that she caught his eyes. "I was just thinking about GiGi. It feels... I don't know... *strange* to be going out having fun when she's in the hospital."

"She wouldn't want us to sit here and mope for her," Sebastian said gently. "If we go early to the beach, we can visit her on the way back..."

Annie tucked her hair behind her ear and bit the inside of her cheek. She wanted *so* badly to go to the beach with Sebastian. But the fact she wanted it so much was making her feel uneasy. She hadn't been in many relationships over the years. Jeremy was probably the most serious and, even with Jeremy, she'd never once felt *excited* to spend time with him. But now, thinking about heading to the coast with Sebastian, on the back of his scooter, with the wind in their hair, was making her stomach flutter almost uncontrollably.

Annie took a deep breath. Then, totally at odds with the voice that was warning her not to get carried away, she said, "Okay, sure. The beach would be lovely."

Sebastian grinned at her and clapped his hands. He seemed excited, and he wasn't trying to hide it. He'd been the same way when he was a teenager... bubbling with energy and just so happy to be spending time with her. Annie remembered it taking her off-guard when they first met. She'd never known *anyone* who carried their feelings so openly and for a long time she'd almost been suspicious of it – until she realised that it was just the way Sebastian was.

Annie smiled, picturing the clear sandy beach, the warm

water, and the cafes along the seafront. "Can we get mussels and chips for lunch?"

For a second, Sebastian frowned at her. And then he let out a loud, booming laugh and slapped his thigh with the palm of his hand. "*Mussels and chips?* You make it sound so horribly British..." He cleared his throat and put on an upper-class accent. "In French we say, '*Moules frites...*'"

Annie blushed and pretended to pout. Sebastian had always loved making fun of her 'uptight' English way of saying things. "I know," she said, rolling her eyes behind her sunglasses. "*Moules frites...*" she gave her best shot at a French accent. "Is that better?"

Sebastian grinned at her, then made an 'okay' sign with his thumb and forefinger, kissed it, and said, "*C'est magnifique, Annie* – very well done."

As the sun began to set over the chateau, Annie and Sebastian had just finished eating a plate of fresh French bread dipped in gloriously rich olive oil when the front gate buzzed, announcing a visitor. Sebastian got up from the table. "It must be Mayor Debois. I'll let her in."

Annie nodded, straightening herself as if she should make an extra special effort to seem presentable. The mayor was an old friend of her grandmother's and extremely important in their small village. Annie had never met her before – or if she had it was so long ago she didn't remember – and when she appeared, Mayor Debois looked nothing like Annie had expected; she was extremely thin with a dark sun-kissed tan, crinkled skin, and long flyaway hair. She was wearing a knee-length linen dress and an enormous smile.

"Annie!" The mayor stepped forward and offered Annie the traditional three-kiss greeting, then she stood back and said, "Your grandmother has shown me pictures over the years, but you are so much lovelier in person. How old were you when you were last here? It has been a long time, yes?"

"Sixteen," added Sebastian. "Annie was last here when she was sixteen."

Annie flinched and looked sideways at him, trying to detect a note of anger or resentment in his voice. But he was still smiling.

"Well, it is wonderful to have you back. And thank goodness you were here for Madame Broudier. What a terrible business. Tell me, how is she?"

As Annie filled the mayor in with details of GiGi's stay in hospital, they slowly walked through the sunroom and out onto the terrace. Now that the sun had almost disappeared, it was cooler. Still humid, but cooler.

"Please," Annie said, gesturing to a chair. "Sit down."

"Oh, thank you." The mayor sighed and flopped down, reaching instantly for a glass of iced tea. "It has been a long day. But, now... we must talk about the festival."

"Yes—" Annie was about to launch into an explanation of why she really felt it was best that they delayed it until GiGi was home from the hospital, because Annie didn't speak French and had absolutely no experience organising events. But she didn't get the chance.

"Your grandmother tells me that you are a very impressive young lady. You own a business, you work with celebrity clients. You are used to *making things happen* as we say."

Annie hesitated. "Yes, that's true, but—"

The mayor clapped her hands. "Then this is fate! It is fate that you are here to help in our hour of need."

Annie glanced at Sebastian, who was clearly trying to hide a snigger behind his glass of iced tea.

"You will do it, Annie, won't you?"

"Do... what?" Annie's eyes widened as the mayor looked at her expectantly.

"Organise the festival for us? I simply don't have time, although of course I will help as much as I can. Your grandmother already has lists of potential vendors who want to bring their food and wine and music. So, it's just a case of contacting them all, organising the decorations and the timings, getting the word out..."

"That sounds like a lot, Mayor Debois and – the thing is – I don't really speak very good French, so I'm not sure—"

"Oh, that's not a problem," Sebastian interrupted. "I can help."

"You can?" Annie's eyebrows tweaked upwards in surprise. "Sebastian you have a busy job, how can you?"

"We'll manage it."

"Really? You will?" The mayor was beaming from ear to ear. "Oh, this is such splendid news. It really is. Saint-Sabran will be so very proud to finally have a festival of our own. We have been talking about it for months, spreading the news amongst the other villages. It would have been such a shame to cancel."

"Of course," Annie said. "Cancelling would be terrible. But... could you not *postpone* it a few weeks?"

The mayor glanced at Sebastian and then laughed. "Oh, but of course we can't. Almost every village in Provence has its own festival over the summer and we chose this time because it does not clash with any of the bigger ones."

"I see." Annie couldn't think of anything that she could say to wriggle her way out of the situation. "And when is the date that you chose?"

"Oh, you have *lots* of time. The festival is going to take place four weeks from today."

Four weeks? To organise a festival that would outshine all other festivals in the area?

Annie swallowed hard. Usually, she approached new and challenging situations with energy and enthusiasm, confident that she could overcome them. But this was different. This was something she was totally uncertain of.

She glanced at Sebastian. Working on the festival together would mean being in close proximity with him for four whole weeks. And, once again, she couldn't make herself say 'no'. So, Annie smiled, clinked glasses with the mayor and told her she'd be happy to help.

CHAPTER 10

SEBASTIAN

They arrived in the small beachside town of Port-le-Rouet just after nine a.m.

Sebastian had set his alarm for six, taken his scooter into the village and collected croissants for breakfast, then returned to the chateau to fill a flask of coffee.

Annie had greeted him by the old water fountain just after seven thirty, and they had set off straight away for the beach.

Leaving early meant they would beat the bank holiday traffic and have enough time to visit Angelique at the hospital on their way back after lunch. But Sebastian also hoped it meant that Port-le-Rouet would be quiet.

On the opposite side of town from the promenade and the restaurants, Sebastian pulled up beside a sloping, rocky bank that led down to the beach and tried to fight the overwhelming realisation that right now – in this moment – teenage-Sebastian's dreams were coming true.

For so many summers, he and Annie had talked about what they would do when Sebastian finally saved enough money to buy a scooter. They had talked about the places they would visit and the places they wouldn't. They had talked about simply driving, for hours, with the wind in their hair.

He had promised her picnics, and music, and paddles in the sea. And she had promised not to schedule every single trip that they took and to enjoy being spontaneous.

Today, fifteen years later, Annie was keeping that promise. She hadn't once asked him where they were going, what time they would get there, how long they'd stay for, or whether he'd thought about where they would eat for lunch.

She had just sauntered down the steps at the front of the chateau, in white cut-offs and a navy-striped blouse, climbed onto the back of the scooter and allowed him to drive away.

Disembarking, Annie slid her sunglasses onto the top of her head and looked up at the sky.

"Not a cloud in sight," she sighed wistfully. Then she turned and smiled at him. "You know, I bet in London it's chucking it down right now."

Sebastian frowned, the usually smooth English-to-French mechanism in his brain faltering. "*Chucking* it down?"

Annie giggled and flicked her ponytail as she tilted her head at him. "Raining really hard."

Sebastian laughed back. "Ah, well. It is England. Of course, it is raining."

Down below them, the sand was white and untouched – washed smooth overnight and not yet covered in footprints from visitors.

Small white waves were licking at the shore and, beyond it, the ocean stretched as far as the eye could see – calm, hypnotic, and dazzlingly blue.

"Wow." Annie breathed out a long, wistful sigh and bobbed

up and down on the soles of her feet.

"Excited to feel the sand between your toes?"

Annie looked down and laughed. "Is it that obvious?"

"Take off your shoes, the path is sandy." Sebastian bent down and slipped off his espadrilles, shoving them into his back pocket and starting to jog. "Last one to the water is a great big loser!"

For a moment, he didn't think she was going to follow him. She just stood there with her hands on her hips, frowning. But then, all of a sudden, she took off. She pushed past him, whooped loudly, and ran full-pelt towards the beach.

Sebastian, of course, had no intention of letting her win. But he did let her get all the way to the water's edge before swinging his arms around her waist and pulling her backwards.

"Sebastian!" Annie shouted. "I won! Come on, I won! You can't–"

But then, somehow, their feet became tangled. Sebastian wobbled and tried to let go of her. Except now she was laughing and fighting him off and their arms were tangled too. And then both of them, together, ended up in a heap, sitting in the foaming waves, soaked to their underwear.

Gallantly, Sebastian stood up and helped Annie to her feet.

Looking down at her almost-see-through trousers, she laughed. "Good job I brought a swimsuit with me, huh?"

Sebastian shook his head and looked back at where they'd ditched their bags before charging into the water. "I brought towels too."

"And food?" Annie asked, expectantly.

"Ah, of course. Food *and* excellent French coffee."

"Can't think of anything better," Annie said, beaming at him.

"Me neither," Sebastian replied. "Me neither."

CHAPTER 11

ANNIE

*A*fter visiting GiGi at the hospital on the way back from Port-le-Rouet, Annie sat down and dangled her feet into the non-existent swimming pool.

She felt sun-weary and dazed from their morning at the beach. She didn't remember the last time she had laughed so hard, or spent time simply *being* rather than *doing*.

Sebastian had been exactly the way he had always been when they were teenagers – bright and relaxed and confident. And Annie had allowed herself to enjoy every second of it.

But the trip to the hospital had sobered her up. GiGi had been chatty and animated, but she had looked tired and the doctors still hadn't given a clear indication of when she'd be allowed to come home.

GiGi had also been extremely concerned about the festival, and insisted that Annie begin organising things *immediately*.

She had reeled off a list of things that Annie would need to do, told her where to find all of her existing notes and correspondence, and asked both of them to please keep her up to date with the developments because she was already bored-silly.

Back at the chateau, Sebastian had gone to finish some work in the old stable and Annie had gathered herself out by the pool – resigned to the fact that she had promised to help and now had to deliver.

In her hands, she held her grandmothers's notebook. GiGi had made extensive notes about everything she'd planned so far for the festival, and Annie was now working her way through them – trying to figure out what she and Sebastian would need to do next.

GiGi had got as far as contacting potential vendors, but it seemed she hadn't firmed anything up with them. Several were marked as 'To Visit', but there were no corresponding appointments sketched into the accompanying calendar, which implied she was yet to arrange a meeting with them.

GiGi didn't do email. Annie found a note which indicated that she'd made contact with a local print centre about making posters, but she couldn't see anything relating to music or potential singers and bands who might like to perform. Annie felt like this was likely to be the biggest challenge; the mayor wanted the festival to take place every night for an entire week, and they would probably need at least two performers per night, which meant *fourteen* musicians would be needed.

The thought gave Annie a lump in her throat and she swallowed it down, tapping her pen on the notebook.

Taking a deep breath and doing what she always did when she was struggling to think straight, she started to make a list of her own. At the very top of the list, she wrote:

Visit a nearby festival.

Despite spending most of her summers in Provence when she was younger, she was certain that the kind of events she'd attended then had grown and changed over the years and, now, she had no idea what to expect from one. Without knowing what she was aiming for, putting together something that would blow the other villages out of the water was going to be extremely difficult.

So, swiping open her phone, she navigated to Google-France and tried to find out when the next local festival would take place. After half an hour of increasingly frustrating searches, she came up blank. Scratching her pen a little too hard on the notebook's surface, next to her first point on the list, she wrote:

Get Sebastian's help!

He had said that he would. But Annie still hadn't really figured out how he was going to manage it when he was working full time. When she'd asked him, he'd merely shrugged it off and laughed – as if it was a joke. As if, of course he'd have time to help her. But Annie knew how important it was – in the early days of setting up a business – to maintain your reputation. If Sebastian started putting people off, cancelling jobs, or shifting them so that he could spend time helping her with her list, it wouldn't do him any favours.

Annie wanted to ask him about it. She wanted to press him for details, but this instinct was something that she'd brought with her from London – the instinct to push and to narrow down details. To find out timings and know exactly when and how things were going to happen. In truth, she had always been that way. And Sebastian never had.

When they were younger, Annie would ask him at the beginning of every day, "What are we doing today Sebastian?" and he would shrug his shoulders and make his little, "Ah..." sound and say, "Whatever we feel like doing." To start with, his attitude had made her feel uneasy. Leaving things to chance didn't come naturally to her, even at ten years old. But every day, and every summer, they had found something fun and unexpected and wonderful to do.

Annie wished that she could still allow herself to be that way, but over the years she'd forgotten the way Sebastian taught her to let go, and she didn't really remember the last time she'd done anything that wasn't planned, or scheduled, or carefully thought out.

Even when she'd made the decision to sub-let her apartment and abscond to Provence for the summer, she had weighed and measured the pros and cons before setting the wheels in motion.

She was adding items to her list when Sebastian appeared behind her.

She knew it was him from his shadow. The way it fell over her and shielded her pasty-white legs from the sun.

"I hope you're wearing sun-screen," he said smoothly, sitting down beside her.

"Of course," she smiled, although she probably should have re-applied it an hour ago.

"Are you making progress?" He glanced at her list and narrowed his eyes at her scrawling handwriting.

"Not really..." Annie frowned and tapped her pen on her temple. "Sebastian, when's the next nearby festival happening? I think I need to visit one because—" She was consulting her list, chewing her lip nervously and tucking her hair behind her ear. But she stopped because Sebastian was laughing at her.

"Of course you do. You need to thoroughly assess the situation and make a plan... am I right?"

Annie tried to look indignantly at him, but softened and rolled her eyes at herself. "Yes. You're right. So—"

"Actually..." Sebastian's eyes lit up. "I believe there is one tonight..."

As sunset approached, Annie stood in the old bridal suite upstairs trying to decide what to wear. Sebastian, of course, would be in his traditional white t-shirt and knee-length denim shorts. But she was finding the decision almost impossible. Everything she'd brought with her felt completely inappropriate – either too flouncy or too 'London'. And the heat was making things even more difficult. The humidity in the area seemed to be rising every day, so anything with sleeves or legs just felt far too claustrophobic.

In the end, she settled on a light blue sun dress and deftly braided her hair so that it was away from her face, scooping it up and pinning it so that wisps fell down in a purposefully messy bun.

In the full heat of the Provence summer, even makeup felt like a layer too much. But the sun and fresh air already seemed to be doing her some good and she was surprised to see that – without the constant grime of the London tube system to contend with – her skin looked healthier than it had in a long time.

Downstairs, Sebastian was waiting for her out front beside his scooter.

As Annie saw him, from the top of the front steps, her heart skipped a beat.

When she went back to England after their last summer together, she had spent almost all of the following year hoping that Sebastian would turn up out of the blue, declare his undying love for her, and sweep her away from her horrid boarding school and lonely life.

Most of the time, this dream had coincided with picturing her school prom. The thought of emerging from her room in a ball gown and seeing Sebastian waiting at the bottom of the stairs had plagued her dreams for months. Probably because of all the fairy tales she'd read growing up, and all the cheesy movies she'd watched.

Of course, Sebastian had never come. Annie had stopped writing to him and ghosted him out of her life, so why in the world would he travel to England to win her back? And, besides, he was barely seventeen at the time and Annie doubted that he'd had enough money for a bus ticket let alone a plane journey.

Nevertheless, she had dreamed and dreamed of him coming to find her and whisk her away.

And now, here he was. All grown up and standing at the foot of the chateau with his wavy hair blowing ever-so-slightly in the breeze. Grinning up at her. Reaching out to take her hand.

As his fingers wrapped around hers, Annie's stomach began to somersault.

"You look lovely," Sebastian said with a smile.

Annie blushed and shook her head a little, batting away the compliment. "I look hot."

Sebastian frowned.

Annie tutted at herself, blushing furiously. "I mean – *temperature* hot. Not…"

Sebastian stopped frowning and started to laugh. "I know what you meant, I was just teasing."

"Of course you were."

Sebastian gestured to the scooter. "Your chariot awaits, dear lady."

The small town of Mimette was about a twenty-minute journey away from Saint-Sabran and Sebastian purposefully drove them through tiny side streets rather than on the motorway to get there.

Clinging on to his firm, steady waist, Annie tried to absorb her surroundings. She had been so familiar with them once, and seeing them again now was a strange combination of *déjà vu* and wonder.

Mimette was a very old town, and one of Annie's favourites because it was enclosed on all four sides by walls and turrets that made it look like an enormous castle.

When they arrived, there were cars and scooters and people *everywhere*. Sebastian parked at the side of the road about half a mile from the town gates. A steady stream of people were walking from their cars to the archways of the town and Sebastian smiled as he saw them. "Wow. It's busy this year," he said. The way he said 'wow', with a funny, rounded emphasis on the 'w' sound, made Annie smile.

"We won't get any closer, I'm afraid." Sebastian climbed off his scooter and helped Annie to follow him.

"That's alright, a walk will be nice."

To start with, the path was too narrow for them to walk side-by-side but as they neared the gates, it widened and Annie felt the sudden urge to slip her hand into Sebastian's. They were walking close to one another. She could feel the warmth of his arm just a fraction away from hers, and she was certain that their fingertips were almost touching.

As they drew closer, she felt as if she was sixteen again – nervous, shy, desperate to say the right thing and make him notice her because for so long she'd been afraid that he thought of her as a friend and not a potential girlfriend.

"You're quiet," Sebastian said, looking at her with a suspicious twinkle in his eye.

"Just taking it all in," she replied. They could hear the music now, and people were milling about in front of the town walls with glasses of wine and cartons of food that smelled divine.

"Are you hungry?" Sebastian noticed her staring at a nearby couple and their carton of fresh oysters.

"Starving, but not for oysters." Annie wrinkled her nose at the thought – slimy, smelly, salty old things. She'd never liked them.

"Ah, but you haven't tried Mimette's oysters."

Annie rolled her eyes at him and continued to walk towards the gate. But then, to her utter disbelief, she realised that Sebastian had approached the oyster-eating couple and was talking at them – quickly – in French. As he finished speaking, all three of them laughed and looked at Annie.

She felt a flush of embarrassment start to creep from her chest to her cheeks. "Sebastian," she whispered, loudly. "What are you doing?"

"Paul and Aurelia are very happy for you to try one of their fantastic Mimette oysters."

"Oh, no, honestly." Annie was mortified. In her part of London, strangers didn't even talk to one another at events like this – let alone share food on request. "Thank you," she said, smiling and nodding and wishing she spoke more than a mere smattering of French. "Thank you, but—"

"Oh, please," the female of the couple beamed, speaking perfect English. "Do try. They are the best for miles around."

Sebastian was looking at Annie expectantly and so was the couple. So, despite the fact her stomach was churning at even the *thought* of eating one, Annie smiled, squeezed some lemon juice onto the raw, grey, glob-like piece of fish... and swallowed it whole.

Even though she didn't chew it, the slime and the salt still managed to coat her tongue and it took every ounce of willpower she had not to gag or spit it out. Gulping it down, she smiled thinly.

"Well...?" Sebastian waved his hands excitedly at her.

"Lovely." She could hardly get the word out. "Best one I've ever had."

The oyster-sharing couple grinned and clapped at her. "Bravo!"

Walking away, as soon as they were out of sight, Annie reached for the water bottle she kept in her handbag and slugged some down.

Beside her, Sebastian was almost shaking with laughter.

"You did that deliberately didn't you?" She put her hands on her hips and glowered at him.

"Ah, maybe." Sebastian shrugged his shoulders at her. "But you did run away and break my poor fragile teenage heart. So, I thought... maybe a little pay-back?"

For a moment, Annie was utterly speechless. Sebastian had said it. Just... said it. And now it was out there she felt like she needed to say something back.

His face was stern and furrowed. But then he began to tremble, holding in a huge holler of a laugh. "Annie..." He pulled her to him and hugged her. "It is a joke." He looked at her and tweaked his forefinger under her chin. "A joke, yes? I was just trying to..." Sebastian trailed off and shrugged.

Annie shook her head at herself, but she couldn't help smiling. "Well, joke or no joke, I'm still hungry, so can we...?"

Sebastian wrapped his arm around her shoulders and squeezed. "Yes, yes we can."

CHAPTER 12

ANNIE

*I*nside Mimette's walls, a cacophony of sights and
sounds greeted them. Craft stalls lined the main
street on both sides. Shops were open late, offering free samples
of ice-cream, pastries, and cheeses. And from the central square,
the sounds of music and laughter drifted towards them.

When they finally reached it, the plaza was full to bursting
with people, lined with trestle tables and huge up-turned barrels
that had been turned into bar-height resting places for wine
glasses and aperitifs.

On three sides, in front of the restaurants and shops, stalls
selling every kind of delicious French food one could imagine
had been set up. There was fresh sea-food, the dreaded oyster
stall, wood-fired pizza, cheese and wine sharing plates, and to
their left a queue that was so long Annie couldn't actually make
out what it was for.

"Ah, that…" Sebastian actually licked his lips. "That is the
onion bhaji lady."

Like, Indian-style bhajis?"

Sebastian nodded, already dragging Annie towards the

queue. "Yes. But made with chickpeas. I don't know how she does it. But she always sells out. We have to get her to come to our festival."

"It's *our* festival now, is it?"

"Of course." Sebastian smiled, again seemingly unfazed by the fact that he had a day job to navigate.

They queued for over twenty minutes. Occasionally, Sebastian would dart off and come back with a glass of wine or a small sharing platter of cheese. But by the time they reached the front of the queue, Annie's stomach was about ready to revolt. It was growling angrily, and she was beginning to think that surely nothing could be worth this amount of waiting.

Finally at the front, Sebastian asked for four bags of bhajis – two each. Annie raised her eyebrows at him, but Sebastian simply nodded with a knowing look on his face.

The bhajis were handed to them in paper cones, a little like the way fish and chips were served at the British seaside. And they retreated to a nearby table to eat them.

Squeezing in between two loud French families and a couple with a large white poodle – who was sitting there like a human, taking up an entire space at the table – Annie and Sebastian sat opposite one another.

Annie looked down at her food and breathed it in. It looked incredible, and smelled even better. Closing her eyes, the way she always did when she was eating something she enjoyed, she savoured every mouthful. And when she looked up, Sebastian was watching her with a funny kind of smile on his face.

"I forgot that you did that," he said, softly.

Annie laughed at herself. "I try not to, but I do it without realising."

"It's cute." Sebastian tweaked the corner of his mouth into a smile that dimpled his cheek and made his jaw look incredibly handsome.

Annie shuffled in her seat, glancing at the people around them in case someone was listening. But, apart from the poodle who was eyeing up her remaining bhajis, no one seemed to be paying them any attention.

Taking a deep breath in, she looked down at her second portion. "Are we really going to eat all of these?"

Sebastian placed his hands palm-down on the table and leaned in as if he was challenging her to a hot-dog eating competition. "I'm man enough... are you?"

"No," Annie replied, dusting off her hands. "But I'm certainly woman enough."

Sebastian grinned. "Then I shall fetch us another drink."

After devouring their double-portion of chickpea bhajis, Sebastian suggested ice cream but Annie simply couldn't manage another mouthful. Instead, she glanced towards the stage.

A blues ensemble had started to play and Annie was watching them longingly. She never had time for music back home. Occasionally, she listened to it on the way to work but more often than not she was catching up on the news or a podcast or emails. And she couldn't remember the last time she'd seen a band live.

Despite the heat in the square, which seemed to be growing even though the sun was setting, Annie was desperate to dance. And, as if he could sense it, Sebastian suddenly rose from the table and gestured for her to follow him.

At the same time, they clambered out from behind the close-together tables and, at the end, Sebastian held out his hand as if he was a prince and she was Cinderella. "*Madamoiselle*, would you care to join me on the dance floor?"

Annie grinned. "*Mai oui*," she replied. "Of course."

"Ah, you are working on your French, I see?" Sebastian nodded approvingly.

Annie shrugged. "I'm picking some more up as I go along, I suppose." She stopped beside one of the large barrels, suddenly keenly aware that no one else was really dancing.

Sebastian walked forwards, then stopped and beckoned for her to follow him. "Come..." he said, enthusiastically.

Annie hesitated. "Maybe we should just stand and listen for a moment."

But Sebastian grabbed hold of her arm and dragged her forwards. The saxophonist smiled at them. The other two people, who were really just swaying slowly rather than dancing, gave them a brief cursory glance. And, to start with, Annie just bobbed a little bit – all of a sudden completely forgetting how to move her feet.

It had been so long since she'd been dancing, let alone to blues music, she had no idea what to do. She felt stiff and awkward and her limbs felt too long. She'd always been conscious of her gangly frame and now it felt even more pronounced than usual. She patted at her hair and looked over her shoulder, trying to think of a reason to go and sit down somewhere.

But then Sebastian grabbed her hand and pulled her close to his chest. His hips were swaying, he slid one hand around her waist and used the other to make her twirl around. And as she looked at him, she started to forget everyone else.

"Do you remember when we used to dance together?" he asked over the music.

Annie laughed. "We made up some pretty terrible dance routines, I seem to recall."

"We certainly did." Sebastian nodded. "But it was fun though, wasn't it?"

Annie looked at him, at his eyes, and smiled. When she thought of Sebastian, that was what she thought of – fun. With him, everything was easy and happy-go-lucky and *possible*.

When they were teenagers, despite the fact he'd come to Saint-Sabran under such horribly sad circumstances when his parents died – or, maybe, *because* he'd suffered something so horrible – he had never taken life too seriously. Sebastian was the embodiment of the phrase 'Live for the Day'. Annie, on the other hand, had taken everything far too seriously.

Annie let herself move closer to him.

The sun had finally set. Twinkling fairy lights had lit up all around the square and the heady scent of wine and food filled the air.

"Annie?" Sebastian now had both hands on her waist, and he had dipped his head so that he was almost whispering in her ear.

Annie held her breath. "Yes?"

Sebastian took a deep breath, paused, then said, "We should definitely hire this band for our festival."

For a moment, Annie didn't move. She couldn't make herself look at him because she was afraid he might see that she'd been hoping he would ask something else. That she had been hoping he would ask to kiss her.

But Sebastian didn't ask, he just stepped away from her, held up his hand and declared, "I am going to speak to them. Wait right there." And, although she was stinging with disappointment, she watched proudly as he charmed the saxophonist into giving him a business card in the middle of their set.

By the time they arrived back at the chateau, it was pitch dark and the moon was shining brightly in the sky. Annie had always marvelled at how clearly the stars could be seen when sitting on the chateau's terrace, and as they paused at the bottom of the front steps she found herself saying nervously, "Would you like to come in and sit out back for a while?"

Sebastian smiled at her. Annie thought he was going to say, *Yes, of course.* But then he rubbed the back of his neck and looked down at his shoes.

"Annie," he said. "I..." He looked up at her and held her gaze for what felt like forever. "I have an early start tomorrow. I should go get some sleep."

Annie instantly straightened herself up and brushed down her dress, flustered and unsure what to say in response – that was the second time in one evening that her feelings had gotten the better of her.

Sebastian leaned forward and kissed her on the cheek. Then waved and used the torch on his phone to light the way to the stable.

Annie watched him go. For a moment, just one brief flash of a moment, she contemplated running after him, grabbing his arm and saying, *There's still something between us, isn't there? Do you feel it too?*

But, of course, she didn't.

CHAPTER 13

SEBASTIAN

*W*alking away from Annie, Sebastian's heart was thundering so loudly in his chest he was almost certain she could hear it.

He almost stopped. He almost turned around, ran back to her, and scooped her up in his arms.

But he didn't.

CHAPTER 14

ANNIE

*T*he staff at the print shop GiGi had visited to discuss
posters did not speak English. Annie had woken
early and called them but had struggled to make them
understand her, so she'd decided to walk from the chateau to the
village. She had thought about knocking for Sebastian at the
stable, but after last night she decided that perhaps some time
alone might be beneficial.

In just a few short days, Annie had found herself
remembering all of the reasons why she'd fallen for Sebastian
when they were teenagers. But last night, as she tossed and
turned and failed to fall asleep, she had been utterly unable to
figure out whether she was remembering how she *used* to feel...
or whether those same feelings were coming back all over again.

If they were – if she was falling for Sebastian the way she
had when she was sixteen – then she needed to find a way to
stop it happening. Her life was in London and Sebastian's was in
France. Nothing had changed.

In fact, if anything, it would be even more impossible for her
to extricate herself from her life in England than it had been

back then. Or for Sebastian to give up his carpentry practice and leave Provence.

In a month's time, just after the festival, she'd be returning to England. So, to avoid being heartbroken again, she needed to put some distance between the two of them. Because, if she was falling for him again – falling for his humour and his warmth and his brightness. If she really could feel her body wanting to be close to him. Then she could also feel that it would all end in disaster. Just like the last time.

No. Annie couldn't allow history to repeat itself. She needed to be sensible and take control of the situation. She needed to create some space between herself and Sebastian. Starting now.

It was a long walk into Saint-Sabran, and it was already smoulderingly hot. By the time Annie reached the river and the bridge that led into the village, her sandals had rubbed a series of uncomfortable blisters into the skin on her heels and she was desperate for both water and coffee.

It had been a long time since Annie had done something by herself for herself. Since she and Jeremy had started the agency, she'd spent most of her 'free' time working or courting clients… which, despite often being in lovely locations like spas or fancy restaurants, was still essentially work.

Before braving the print shop – she hoped she could get them to understand her with the help of Google Translate – Annie stopped by the river and purchased a coffee from one of the small cafes nearby.

She drank it at a table overlooking the water, and the mere fact that she was alone and that she wasn't having to talk to anyone or impress anyone was remarkably freeing. She wasn't wearing makeup, she wasn't dressed to impress, and she wasn't trying to make herself appear funny or confident or powerful. She was just Annie. Sitting there with her own thoughts, smiling at the way the clouds were reflected on the surface of the river.

She was about to get up and try to finally locate the printer's, when she felt someone's presence behind her. Looking up, of course, it was Sebastian.

"You left very early," he said, with a note of surprise in his voice.

"I called the printer's and they couldn't understand me, so I thought I'd come and try to make myself understood in person."

Sebastian chuckled. "Oh yes, and how will you do that?"

Annie waved her phone at him. "The wonders of technology."

"I'll come with you." Sebastian sat down opposite her and motioned for the waitress to bring another coffee. "Just as soon as I've had my caffeine."

"You're not working?" Annie shuffled in her chair.

"I have some jobs this afternoon. Nothing much."

Annie couldn't tell whether Sebastian was telling the truth of not, and he quickly changed the subject.

"Did you email the band from last night?"

"Yes," Annie replied, glancing down at her phone and wrinkling her nose. "They haven't replied yet, though."

Sebastian laughed and placed his hands palm-down on the table, reaching them towards her as if he might be about to entwine his fingers with hers.

Annie leaned back and tucked her hands into her lap.

"Give them a chance, Annie. It has been less than twenty-four hours. I know things move quickly in London but here in the South of France we are a little more... relaxed."

Annie smiled knowingly. "Well, that's certainly true."

"And is that a bad thing?" Sebastian was watching her carefully, as if he was trying to figure out whether she was being playful or whether she genuinely found the slower pace irritating.

"No. Not at all."

Sebastian nodded, then leaned back and sighed at the river. "This is one of my favourite spots for coffee," he said. And, as if he had tempted fate, the waitress appeared behind him with a mug of espresso. Sebastian downed it in one, put some Euros down on the table and stood up. "This way," he said, sauntering off towards a street a little way from the village square.

Annie hesitated. Part of her wanted to bound up beside him like an excited puppy, bubbling with enthusiasm. But a bigger part – the part that had only minutes ago decided she was going to remember that they could never be anything more than friends – was telling her to restrain herself. So, she casually walked beside him, glancing occasionally at her notebook and trying *not* to think about how handsome he looked in the sunshine.

CHAPTER 15

ANNIE

TWO WEEKS LATER

It was late afternoon. Annie had been staring at the chateau's business accounts for hours, and her mind was swimming. The study was incredibly hot and making her brain feel foggy and sluggish. She'd tried opening the shutters, hoping for even the hint of a breeze to waft through and cool the beads of sweat at the nape of her neck. But they had simply let in more light and allowed the temperature to climb even higher.

Checking her phone for the local weather, it told her it was thirty-eight degrees but felt like forty-two. Annie clunked the phone down sharply on the desk in front of her, taking her frustration out on it because if she didn't she might start ripping up sheets of paper or crumpling them into balls and hurling them at the waste-paper basket.

She had looked at the chateau's accounts for the last four years, going back before her grandfather had died. And she'd discovered that, actually, the problems had started long before his death. GiGi had told her not to worry, to focus on the festival but – knowing that her grandmother was thinking of selling up – Annie simply couldn't leave it alone.

Closing the folder in front of her, she sighed and scraped her fingers through her hair.

Examining the books, it was clear what had gone wrong; as her grandparents had gotten older, they'd refused to take on the level of help they needed. The chateau had fallen into more and more disrepair, bookings for wedding and large corporate events had stopped, and then the money had stopped too. And now, her grandmother was stuck. There were no bookings scheduled to bring money in and there wasn't enough cash to do all of the work that was needed to *bring* bookings in.

Annie had done all of the calculations. But the chateau was in limbo, and Annie couldn't see a way out of it. She'd even considered injecting some cash herself, but the amount the chateau needed was too much even for her, especially if she considered that GiGi would need to hire a chef, a grounds keeper, an on-site maintenance man, and an events coordinator.

If they opened up the chateau's grounds for tourists as well as events, that could provide an extra stream of income. But, again, it would require improvements and alterations.

The only solution Annie could think of was the kind of investment that had helped her and Jeremy get their business off the ground back in London – a silent investor who would stump up the cash and take a percentage of the profits, as well as a stake in the property, going forward.

If she could write up a solid business plan, it might just work. A silent investor would allow GiGi to keep control of the property, and losing a little bit of the equity in the building and the business was, surely, better than losing the chateau altogether.

So, ignoring the voice in her head that was still unbelievably angry with Jeremy, Annie opened up her laptop and navigated to her emails.

Jeremy,

I'm sorry I left so suddenly. After everything that happened, I needed some space to clear my head.

I know you'll be taking care of the business. I appreciate you stepping in and respecting the fact that I asked for some peace and quiet and not to be bothered with work while I'm here.

I'm not sure when I will be back. I have some urgent family business to fix before I can return. Which is why I'm emailing you.

My grandparents' chateau is in financial trouble. Since Grandpa died, GiGi hasn't been coping and the place has fallen into disrepair. I've been looking things over and I think I could draw up a solid business plan that would attract investors.

I know you've got contacts at Jarold's, so I was wondering whether you might put some feelers out and see if there's any interest before I investigate further?

I appreciate this is a big ask, especially given the way I left. But I hope you know me well enough by now to understand that I wouldn't have taken the time out if I didn't think it was best for the agency. I needed space to recalibrate, and I think you did too.

Let me know what you think about the chateau. I haven't mentioned anything to GiGi yet, so at this stage it's all hypothetical, but I can't leave until I've come up with some kind of solution for her. I'm really hoping that solution doesn't involve selling up. It would break her heart. And mine.

Best wishes,

Annie

Signing off her email with 'Best Wishes' felt extremely odd, and so did the slightly grovelling tone she'd adapted. But Jeremy had always responded well to that kind of thing. So, Annie gritted her teeth and pressed send.

If Jeremy came back with some positive feelings from his friends at Jarold's, she would talk to her grandmother and draw up a business plan.

If he didn't, then Annie would have to face the fact that selling was the only option they had left.

CHAPTER 16

SEBASTIAN

*S*ebastian found Annie in her grandmother's study. Angelique had been in hospital for two whole weeks and, although he hadn't admitted it, he had missed her terribly.

Angelique and Michael Broudier had been like parents to Sebastian when he moved to Saint-Sabran. His aunt had taken him in, but Angelique and Michael were the ones who had really *cared* for him.

Since he had moved into the old stable at the chateau and started to convert it into both his home and his workshop, he had seen Angelique at least once a day. And now that she wasn't there, it was reminded Sebastian just how awful it would be if she was forced to sell.

He knew that Annie was determined to find a way to prevent it from happening. She had been holed up in the study for hours, poring over the accounts. But, even though he knew how brilliantly business-minded she was, Sebastian was not hopeful that she'd find a solution.

Even *he* could see that the numbers would not add up.

Which meant that, in all likelihood, by the end of the year he would lose his home.

He would also, he was certain of it, lose Annie.

When she had first arrived, he had been determined not to fall for her again. Absolutely resolute that he would not allow his heart to be broken.

But within days, he had weakened.

The beach, the festival in Mimette, dancing together to blues music – it had all been too much for his heart to resist.

That night in Mimette, he had wanted nothing more than to pull her close and kiss her and never let her go again. But he had stopped himself. And, since then, he felt like she had been pulling away from him.

At the beach, when they were paddling in the crystal blue waters, and in Mimette, when they were eating and dancing and drinking wine, Sebastian had been certain that the spark between them was mutual – that Annie wanted him as much as he wanted her.

But something had changed. After he walked away from her that night, she drew back from him. Sebastian could feel it – a veil had been drawn between them – and he wasn't sure how to navigate past it.

He wanted to tell her that the reason he'd pulled away was because it was all just too much, too soon. Because he couldn't quite believe she was back in Provence and because he was terrified of falling for her again and having to say goodbye. But he couldn't find the words, so instead he had spent the last two weeks trying to bring back the Annie he'd danced with that night by just being... himself.

He had moved work around, made time to help her with the festival, made her laugh. They had spent the evenings eating and talking together on the terrace. And she had been friendly, warm, funny and open.

She had told him about her life in England, the agency she had started with her ex-boyfriend Jeremy who, she said, she'd had a narrow escape from.

She had talked to him about the celebrities she'd met through her work, about Borough Market and Tower Bridge and the eclectic mix of people that made London one of the most amazing places in the world.

But she hadn't mentioned what had happened between them, all those years ago. She hadn't explained why she left, or why she stopped writing to him. And she hadn't looked at him the way she did when they were dancing in Mimette.

Now, he was almost beginning to think that he'd been imagining it. Perhaps she hadn't looked at him that way. Perhaps, even if she had, it was best that they kept things neutral – no more than friends – because in a few weeks she'd be flying back to London.

But, Sebastian couldn't help it. Despite his head telling him to be sensible and carry on as they were, his heart was shouting something different. His heart wanted Annie – *needed* Annie. So, he decided to give it one last shot.

"Annie?" As he stuck his head around the door of Angelique's study, he waved and smiled broadly.

Annie looked up from the desk, sighed and pulled her hair away from her neck.

"Any luck?"

She shook her head and looked at the paperwork in front of her. "No. I'm afraid not."

Sebastian walked across the room and perched on the lip of one of the large windows that looked out onto the front driveway. "I think maybe a break is in order."

Annie's nose wrinkled as she considered what he'd said. "What kind of break?"

"Well, we still have vendors to secure for the festival. We have booked music and food but we need some local craft too I think."

Annie sighed again. For the first time since she'd arrived, she looked on the verge of being overwhelmed by everything. So, Sebastian quickly strode over and spun her chair around to face him.

Placing his hands lightly on her arms, he bobbed down and grinned at her. "Come on. It'll be fun."

"Fun?"

"Ah, well, you said you always wanted to see the lavender fields..."

Annie's eyes brightened a little.

"There's a woman I have heard about. She weaves the most incredible things from lavender. She has a workshop towards the fields near Aix. We could visit her? And take a walk through the lavender?" As he spoke, Sebastian could feel his throat tightening. Walking through the lavender fields was something they had always dreamed of doing together. Annie had talked endlessly about it when they were teenagers and it had been first on their list of places to visit once Sebastian finally bought his scooter.

Annie closed her eyes and breathed in deeply. Sebastian wished he could tell what she was thinking. For a moment, he thought she was going to say no. But then he saw her shoulders relax a little, and the muscles in her face began to un-tense. "Alright," she said, opening her eyes and smiling at him. "That sounds wonderful."

CHAPTER 17

ANNIE

Sebastian stopped the scooter in front of a small, unassuming, grey stone farmhouse. Unclipping the helmet he kept forcing her to wear, Annie tied it onto the handlebars and pushed her sunglasses onto the top of her head.

Looking around, she frowned. "I don't see many swathes of purple..."

"Ah," Sebastian grinned. "That's because *these* fields are one of Provence's best kept secrets."

"Secret lavender fields?"

Sebastian nodded solemnly, but then winked at her and said, "*Mai oui*... but of course! Most of the fields here have become tourist spots. But *these* fields – Madame Gerrard's fields – are hidden. Super special." He reached out and took her hand. "Come. This way."

Annie almost took her hand back. The sudden, intimate, contact made her heart do a somersault and, since the festival in Mimette, she had been trying so very hard not to feel at all... somersault-y.

But once her skin met Sebastian's, she found she couldn't make herself break away from him.

Sebastian knocked on the door of the farmhouse and a short middle-aged man answered.

Sebastian spoke quickly, in French, and the man nodded, grinned, nodded some more, then gestured for them to step inside.

The centre of the farmhouse was cool and dark, with low ceilings and stone walls.

The man who answered the door showed them through a large hallway and a series of arches, then suddenly they were outside again.

Annie stopped. Her breath caught in her chest and she heard herself whisper, "Oh, my."

In front of them, fields and fields of vivid purple lavender stretched almost as far as she could see. Set slightly below the farmhouse, from the road, they had been utterly obscured by the stone wall surrounding the property. But now there they were... like something from a travel magazine. Rows and rows of splendid colour.

Annie turned to Sebastian and grinned. "Seb..." She almost called him by his nickname, but then corrected herself. "Sebastian... this is incredible."

"Would you like to take a walk?" he asked. He was still holding her hand.

"Yes. I really would."

At the bottom of the slope behind the farmhouse, they entered the lavender field. Stepping between the rows, Annie stretched out her arms and grinned.

She turned to Sebastian and he was watching her carefully. He was standing one row over and the glint in his eyes told her he was about to do something mischievous.

But then he simply took out his phone and held it up. "I need to capture this," he said. "For a memory."

Annie felt her smile falter. "For a memory?"

Sebastian was still holding the phone up, gesturing for her to pose. "Yes, hold out your arms again."

"That's what you always used to say..."

Sebastian lowered the phone. He was still smiling but his eyes were searching her face. "Yes, I suppose I did."

"We made a lot of memories, didn't we?" Annie was remembering the box under the bed.

"And we can make lots more." Sebastian blinked quickly, as if he was shrugging off the seriousness of the moment, and then waggled his phone at her again. "Come on... arms out."

Annie smiled and rolled her eyes, but did as she was told. Then she said, "Let's take one together... a selfie."

Sebastian laughed. "Were selfies invented back when we were kids?"

"No. I don't think they were."

"Then we have lots of time to make up for." Sebastian squeezed in close to her so that both of their faces filled the screen. Then, just as he was about to press capture, he turned and kissed her firmly on the cheek.

Annie was so taken by surprise that she almost gasped. And when they looked at the photograph, she had a comical raised-eyebrow expression on her face.

"You look horrified," Sebastian laughed.

Annie shook her head. She was laughing too. But then she found herself saying, "I could never be horrified to be kissed by you."

Sebastian didn't look at her. He was still holding the phone and staring at it as if he didn't dare move. Nervously, he cleared his throat.

Annie breathed in slowly. He was so close to her that her skin was flickering, as if it was about to catch light.

She didn't want to ruin the moment. She didn't want to take away the possibility that he might turn to her and kiss her and tell her he'd been going crazy since the moment she arrived back in France.

But all of a sudden, she knew she needed to tell him the truth. She had to tell him why she abandoned him the way she did. Why she never came back. Why she broke his heart.

CHAPTER 18

ANNIE

"Seb..." This time, she didn't correct herself and use his full name. She allowed the word *Seb* to just settle there, between them, sounding exactly the way it used to.

"*Oui?*"

"I want to explain to you what happened that summer." She looked down at the dusty path between the lavender bushes and scuffed her toe against it. "I want to apologise."

Sebastian slid his phone into his pocket and looked at her. His mouth had settled into the same almost-smile that it always did, but his eyes were still and watching her carefully.

Annie took a deep breath. "I handled things very badly. I was young, and I know that's not an excuse but... well, now I'd do things very differently."

"Annie, you don't have to—"

"I want to. I try not to have any regrets in life. I believe everything happens for a reason. I like who I am, and I wouldn't be this person if things had gone a different way. But I will *always* regret the way I left. I'll always regret the way I treated you. And I'll always, *always* regret not writing you back."

Sebastian took his sunglasses from where they were perched on top of his head and picked thoughtfully at them. "Why didn't you?"

Annie sighed. This was it. Truth time.

"You remember when I wrote to you before I arrived, and I told you I was going to ask my parents if I could come to live in France?"

Sebastian nodded. "Of course."

"And when I arrived that summer I told you that they had agreed?"

Sebastian smiled a little. "Yes. We spent many, many hours talking about it, Annie. Talking about what we'd do and how wonderful it would be–"

Annie closed her eyes, almost wincing at the excited nostalgia in his voice. "The thing is, Sebastian. It was all a lie."

When she opened them, Sebastian was frowning at her.

"I knew before I came here that summer that my parents wouldn't allow me to move to France. I asked them before I even wrote to you about the idea. I begged and pleaded with them for weeks, but they were adamant. They said they'd poured thousands into my private education and wouldn't let me throw it away. They said it would take me too long for my French to get up to scratch and my grades would suffer." She tried to laugh a little, because if she didn't she might start crying. "It was all very dramatic."

Sebastian breathed in slowly and his nostrils flared in a way that Annie hadn't seen before.

"Sebastian, I—"

"If you knew they wouldn't allow it, why did you let me believe it might happen? Why did you go along with it all summer? The pretence and the dreaming and all the plans we made?" Sebastian sounded the closest to angry that Annie had ever heard him. And yet, still, he looked as if he wanted to pull her close and kiss her forehead and tell her everything would be okay.

Annie swallowed hard. She had never spoken her reasons out loud before. She'd never even really admitted them to herself before. "Because I wanted it so badly that it was like a physical pain in my belly – every single day. Boarding school in England was *miserable*. All I wanted was to be here with you. I was sixteen and I was *so* in love with you. And I just wanted one glorious summer where I could pretend everything was going to be okay." She was speaking quickly, the subtle scent of the lavender field only just managing to calm her down. "You went through so much when you were younger, Sebastian. And I know my troubles in a silly English boarding school are nothing compared to that, but I was so lonely. And I really did love you. And–"

Sebastian reached out and put his hand on her forearm. "I loved you too." His eyes were so blue, so perfect... just like they were back then. He smiled and took his hand away, his cheeks dimpling into a gentle smile. "But we were kids, Annie. I don't blame you for what happened." He sighed and shook his head. "Sure, okay, maybe you could have handled it better but – my goodness – I did many silly things when I was sixteen." Sebastian shrugged, as if it was all water under the bridge. "We're different people now. It's all in the past."

Annie blinked at him. All these years, she'd carried around an enormous, heavy boulder of guilt for the way she'd treated Sebastian. But now she'd finally told him the truth, he seemed... *okay* with it.

"Besides, as you said – if things had happened differently, you wouldn't have built your amazing life in London." Sebastian had started walking back towards the farmhouse. Still smiling, still friendly. But not holding her hand.

"Oh, I'm not sure it's all that amazing." She wanted to open up to him about Jeremy, and the business, and her doubts about her big city life. But Sebastian nudged her playfully and said, "Of course it is. You made your own business, from scratch. An amazing business. You should be *very* proud."

Annie reached up and fumbled for her sunglasses, unsure whether she wanted to wear them because of the glaring mid-day sun or because she didn't want Sebastian to see her expression. "It's really not that impressive. I wasn't alone. Jeremy was there too and, to be honest, none of it would have happened if we hadn't secured investment when we were starting out."

"Investment?" Sebastian slid his sunglasses back on too and bent to pick a spring of lavender. He held it under his nose, sniffing it gently.

Annie sighed as the conversation settled into something normal and friendly and very far away from what she'd hoped it would be after she bared her soul to him. "When we started the company, Jeremy and I were working for this huge firm called Fox PR. We'd worked our way up, we were both managing important accounts and we had clients we knew would follow us if we left. But we didn't have nearly enough money to start things up." She breathed in slowly, remembering the stress and the excitement and the adrenaline rush she'd felt back then. "We'd been turned down by pretty much every avenue we'd tried. We couldn't get a big enough loan and investors didn't want to know."

"But then you found someone?"

"A silent investor through a small European firm. Without that money, we'd never have even got off the ground."

"Annie," Sebastian tutted, "it doesn't matter whether you

had a loan, or an investor, or a genie from a lamp or a fairy Godmother. You still built something incredible. I am very proud of you."

Annie looked sideways at Sebastian. Very few people had told her they were proud of her, and the compliment felt strangely intimate. "Thank you."

Again, he shrugged as if it was no big deal. Then, changing the subject, he said, "Okay, have you seen enough lavender?"

Annie smiled. "I don't think it's possible to ever see *enough* of these lavender fields."

That evening, Annie arrived back at the chateau feeling as if a weight had been lifted from her shoulders. She had told Sebastian the truth and the day had carried on as normal. He hadn't been angry, or upset. And now, thinking about it, she couldn't quite believe that she'd expected him to be. This was Sebastian – *Seb* – always smiling, always looking on the bright side, always seeing the good in people. Of course he wasn't angry with her for being a confused teenager and making some mistakes fifteen years ago.

But one weight had been replaced by another, less heavy, niggling weight. Because, despite opening up and telling him what had really happened, the rest of the afternoon had continued just like every other afternoon for the past two weeks – completely uneventfully.

They had spoken to the lavender craftswoman about coming to the festival. She had agreed and recommended some friends who would also like to take part. They had stopped by the hospital, updated GiGi, and given her a bouquet of lavender to put beside her bed.

They had collected fresh bread and salad from the village.

And they'd returned to the chateau to make dinner, cooking together and eating together and being normal and friendly.

But sitting opposite Sebastian as the sun was about to set, watching the horizon turn a deep shade of orange and feeling the air finally begin to cool, Annie realised that she didn't want normal. And she didn't want friendly.

She wanted Sebastian.

So, when they went back inside to fetch coffee, she told him she'd be right back, bounded up the stairs to her old bedroom and scrabbled under the bed for the memory box she'd found on her first day back. Stroking the lid, she smiled. Now was the time. The time for them to open it up and go through it together.

But when she stepped into the kitchen, before she had a chance to take the box out from behind her back and say, *Tah Dah!* Sebastian patted her on the arm and said, "I'm sorry, Annie. I have to go. I forgot I have a visitor."

"A visitor?"

"*Oui.* I will see you tomorrow, yes?"

Annie opened her mouth to ask if he'd be coming back later, but he was already rushing back towards the front door. And then he was gone. So, she spent the evening alone. And, sitting outside looking up at the clear starry sky, she realised that this was the first night she'd been completely by herself since she'd arrived in Saint-Sabran.

Back in London, Annie was alone pretty much every night. When she returned home from the office, it was just her and the T.V. and a take out meal. Even when she and Jeremy had been dating, all it really meant was that they'd gone out for dinner together, occasionally the theatre. But still, she'd gone home alone every night and woken up alone every morning. She had so much time alone with her own head, and so very little time actually talking to other people.

Somehow, she'd found herself a thirty-year-old woman with a fantastic career but no friends and no family nearby.

And that was how her parents had always been. They weren't the kind of parents who chatted to Annie and her brother Tommy over dinner each night, who played boardgames and went on family outings. They were the kind who called the boarding school each weekend to check everything was *okay* and who did their best to organise trips abroad – with a nanny – or summers in France with the grandparents so that they didn't really have to be around their children.

Her parents loved her, she knew that. But it wasn't the warm TV advert kind of love that she got from her grandmother. And it wasn't the kind of love Sebastian had had with his parents when they were alive.

Annie had always thought that the reason Sebastian was so open about his feelings was because he knew just how quickly life could change – he knew that if you wanted someone to know how you felt, you should say it. Just in case you didn't get another chance.

And being back here with him and spending so much time together over the last few weeks – even if it was just riding on his scooter to the hospital or visiting the market at the weekend – had reminded her why she'd wanted so badly to come and live here when she was younger.

She had wanted the warmness. Not just the physical warmth of the sun, and the laid back feeling that embodied the towns and villages nearby; she'd wanted the warmth that you feel when you have a community of people around you who genuinely care.

And suddenly, washing over her like a tsunami, Annie

realised that all this time she had been so very lonely. All this time, she'd cut herself off from France and Sebastian and her grandparents because the contrast was too painful. Because they reminded her too much of what she'd lost.

Standing up, she reached for the memory box and looked down towards Sebastian's house. Taking a deep breath, she walked down the steps and towards the woods.

She was smiling to herself, with the memory box tucked under her arm, when she caught a glimpse of the old stable. She stopped and took a deep breath. But before she could move forwards, she heard voices. Sebastian's door opened, and a woman stepped out. A woman with long black hair, cut off jeans, and a beaming smile.

Sebastian kissed her on the cheek. Once, twice, three times, *four* times. And then they embraced. He wrapped his arms around her.

Annie couldn't watch. She felt sick to her stomach. She wavered for a moment, looking down at the floor. And then she turned and ran back to the chateau.

CHAPTER 19

ANNIE

The following morning, Annie left the house before Sebastian woke up. She borrowed her grandmother's car and drove to the hospital. The entire way, she felt as if she was about to career off the side of the road – or into an oncoming vehicle – at any moment. She stalled three times, at busy roundabouts, but finally she made it.

As soon as GiGi saw her, she frowned and pushed herself up on her pillows. "You came alone, Annie?"

Annie sat down and wiggled the keys at her. "Yes, I thought it was about time I got the hang of driving over here."

GiGi nodded, but didn't reply, as if she knew that staying quiet would force Annie to keep speaking and tell her what was really going on.

Annie breathed in, then sat back in the plastic hospital chair and scraped her hair back into a loose top-knot. "I didn't want to speak to him this morning."

"Have you two had an argument?" GiGi asked, knowingly.

"Not exactly..." Annie fiddled with the keys for a moment,

then looked up and said, "GiGi, do you know if Sebastian is dating anyone?"

"You mean if he has a girlfriend?" Her grandmother seemed surprised. "Not that I know of. There was a girl from the village last year, I believe, who he was very close to, but…" She paused and tutted loudly. "Now, Annie. Don't tell me you're getting jealous?"

Annie flinched and felt her cheeks start to flush. "No. Not jealous, just… I saw him last night. Late. A woman was leaving the stable. He kissed her on the cheeks and—"

"Well," GiGi threw up her good hand and rolled her eyes. "We all do that… if cheek-kissing was a sign of being in a relationship then the entire population of Provence would be in serious trouble."

Annie tried to smile, but then a little quieter she added, "He hugged her too."

Her grandmother looked at her for a moment, and then laughed. A slow chortling laugh that reminded Annie of a teapot boiling. "Annie, dear. I'm not sure that's enough to imply she's his girlfriend. And, besides, even if she *is*… what's wrong with that?"

GiGi was challenging Annie to be honest about her feelings, but she wasn't ready. She couldn't say it out loud. "Nothing, I suppose."

Her grandmother sighed and patted the edge of the bed. Annie moved over and sat beside her. "Annie, do you know why I never told you what Sebastian was up to all these years? Why I didn't keep you informed, tell you he was still living here and training as a carpenter? Or that he'd got his first job, his first car, started his own business…?"

Annie shook her head.

"Because you can't have your cake and eat it."

Annie frowned.

Kindly, GiGi said, "You broke his heart, Annie. He had very little joy in his life after his parents died, and then he moved here to live with his aunt and he met you. This scrawny, shy, blonde little thing from England. And you changed everything for him. Every summer he was more and more excited for your arrival. And then you told him you were coming to live here, and I could see it in his face – it was all of his dreams come true." GiGi sighed and shook her head. "I probably should have said something myself. I thought it was out of character for your parents to have agreed, but I suppose I liked seeing you both so happy."

Annie could feel tears threatening the back of her eyes. "It wasn't *your* fault, GiGi. I wanted it to be true so badly. But I broke his heart because I left."

"Not just because you left. You left without an explanation. You left and you never spoke to him again. And you stayed away for fifteen years."

Annie wiped a tear from her cheek and hung her head.

Her grandmother squeezed her hand. "I know that you didn't write or visit or call for all those years because you were heart broken too." She breathed in and looked Annie very carefully in the eyes. "*But* you still left. So, it wouldn't have been fair for me to tell you about Sebastian's life. Do you see?"

Annie wiped her eyes with the back of her hand. "Yes."

"And if Sebastian *does* have a girlfriend..."

"Then I have no right to be upset about it?"

GiGi shrugged. "I'm not saying you shouldn't be upset. But Sebastian has a big heart, Annie. And he still cares for you deeply."

"So, you're saying that I shouldn't tell him how I feel?"

"Oh no, of *course* you should tell him." GiGi's expression

was resolute. "But only if you're certain... are you certain, Annie?"

Annie opened her mouth to answer. But nothing came out. Was she certain? Or was being back in Provence making her feel things that weren't really there? If she went back to England, back to London and the business and Jeremy, would she forget about Sebastian? Or would she be heart-broken all over again?

Despite the fact she'd spent her first two weeks back in Provence telling herself that she had no choice, that there was no way she and Sebastian could be together even if they wanted to be, in reality there was no one stopping her from leaving England. If she really wanted to, she could make it happen. She could fly back and forth for work, run the business via email and Skype. Jeremy would never let her quit, but maybe she could take a step back and hire someone to take her place...?

But what if she told Sebastian that she didn't want to leave and, instead of wrapping his arms around her and begging her to stay, he told her to go? What if she cut all ties with London and things didn't work out? What if their romance was simply meant to stay in the past?

CHAPTER 20

SEBASTIAN

*A*s Marguerite walked back up the path towards the chateau, Sebastian turned and smiled to himself. Finally, he could finish the project he'd been working on for over fifteen years. Finally, he could finish the gift that he'd begun making for Annie when they were sixteen years old.... after their first – and only – kiss in the storm.

He had started working on it again just after she arrived. It had stood in the corner of his workshop ever since he'd moved into the old stable. Many times, he had looked at it and contemplated finishing it. He never had. But when he went back to the stable that first night, after they walked through the woods together, he'd experienced the overwhelming need to complete it.

At first, he thought he was just doing it because it was a nice gesture or because it would enable him to show her how talented he was. But now he knew that wasn't the reason – he knew he was doing it because he wanted to show Annie what she meant to him. He needed a gesture. A big gesture. And even after finding out that she had lied to him, that there had never been

130

any possibility of her moving to France, his feelings hadn't changed.

If anything, they had grown stronger.

For so long, he thought that Annie had abandoned him because she didn't feel as strongly as he did. Because she didn't love him as much as he loved her. Because she changed her mind and decided she would be better off without him.

But that wasn't what happened – Annie cut him out of her life because she loved him *too* much. She lied about moving to France because she wanted it so badly. And she had been feeling guilty about it ever since.

At first, when she told him, standing there in the middle of a field of lavender and looking unbelievably beautiful in a long white dress, Sebastian had felt angry. He'd remembered all the times they had talked about what would happen when she moved in with her grandparents and how excited she was to leave her dreadful boarding school. They'd even talked about how she had managed to persuade her parents to allow it. But all of those conversations had been nothing more than make-believe. All that time, Annie knew it wasn't really going to happen. But she didn't say anything.

Sebastian had stayed angry for longer than he'd let her see. His instinct to protect her being stronger than his need to vent. But as the afternoon drew on, he softened. And by the time they arrived back at the chateau, he had forgiven her entirely.

When Marguerite called and told him she was close by, it felt like fate – the perfect time to finish his gift and prove to Annie that he'd never stopped thinking about her.

Brushing his hands down on his shorts, he shrugged to loosen his shoulder muscles, then stretched his hands out in front of him.

Annie was going to love it...

CHAPTER 21

ANNIE

*A*nnie didn't return to the chateau until the evening. The sun was turning orange and getting ready to dip down below the horizon. The air was dusky and humid. She had spent the entire afternoon walking – walking through Saint-Sabran, walking by the river, walking and thinking about Sebastian.

GiGi had asked her if she was *certain* of how she felt about Sebastian. But the truth was, even after hours of trying to figure it out, she still wasn't.

It was all too mixed up. Her memories from their childhood summers together, her heightened emotions about the chateau being sold, her confusion about the life she'd left behind in London.

So when she returned, instead of trying to find Sebastian, she walked up the front steps of the chateau with the intention of going straight upstairs – hoping that sleep would help her put her feelings in some kind of order.

She sighed and shrugged her bag off her shoulder, resting it with a thud on the console table near the staircase.

Then she looked up.

In the centre of the entrance hall, highlighted by a dusty beam of sunlight streaming in from the windows above the stairs, sat a large, wooden rocking horse.

A trickle of electricity ran from Annie's neck all the way to her toes. Her hand went to her mouth to stifle an, "Oh, my..."

She walked over to the horse and let her fingers stroke the smooth curve of its back. She knew this rocking horse. It looked exactly like...

"Does it look like him?" Sebastian appeared from the sunroom. He was smiling at her but looked nervous, holding his hands behind his back and dipping his head as if he was scared of her answer.

Annie could feel tears welling up behind her eyes. "It's Monty, isn't it?"

Sebastian's smile widened. "So, I captured his likeness?"

Annie's hand was now resting on the horse's mane. She nodded. The rocking horse was a perfect replica of the horse she'd had as a child. The horse she'd been forced to leave behind when her parents sent her to boarding school. The horse she'd told Sebastian about so many times.

"I always promised you that I'd find a way of bringing him back to you. I know it not the real Monty but..."

Sebastian didn't get a chance to finish his sentence because Annie hurled herself towards him and wrapped her arms around his neck. She was crying, but she didn't care. She nuzzled into him and whispered, "Thank you, thank you, thank you."

When she finally let go of him, she looked from Sebastian to the rocking horse and back again.

"How did you... I mean, *when* did you?"

Sebastian walked over to the horse and patted its flank. Bashfully, without looking at her, he replied, "I began it when we were sixteen. After our last summer together." He cleared his throat and looked up. "Do you remember, that night in the storm, when we..."

Annie began to blush. The night they shared their first and only kiss, they had spent hours talking about what they would do when they were older. All the things they would see. They had talked about having a family of their own and...

"We said that when we were older, and married, and running the chateau together, we would let our children ride horses all day long." Sebastian paused and looked at her. "I wanted to make you this as a... gesture. For when you returned. To welcome you back."

"But then I never came back..." Annie almost whispered it because the thought of Sebastian waiting and waiting and working on this beautiful gift was making her heart hurt.

Sebastian shrugged, "Ah, no. You didn't. So, I stopped working on him. But after I collected you from the airport, I knew I had to finish it." He laughed a little and stroked the horse's tail. "It was nearly ready days ago, but I had to wait for my friend Marguerite to bring me the horse hair. I wanted it to be real horse hair."

Annie's eyes widened. "Marguerite? Your friend?"

"*Oui*," Sebastian replied casually.

Annie looked down at her sandals and shook her head at herself. "She came here last night?"

"Yes." Sebastian was looking at her as if he wasn't sure why she was asking, but then his eyes widened. "You saw her?"

"I did." Annie's cheeks were flushing pink and her skin felt prickly as she remembered the knot in her stomach when she saw Sebastian embrace his friend. "I thought..."

Sebastian stepped closer and dipped his head to meet her eyes. "What did you think?"

"I thought she was your girlfriend."

Sebastian smiled slowly, the corner of his lip curling ever-so-slightly, the way it always did. "And what did you think about that?"

"I felt *awful*." Annie sighed as she spoke. Saying it out loud, she felt a whoosh of tension release from her chest. "I hated the thought of it, Sebastian. And I know that I've no right to feel that way, but..."

"Annie..." Sebastian reached out and took her hand in his, stroking her palm with his thumb as he spoke. "You don't need to worry. And do you know why?"

Annie shook her head. She couldn't speak. Her heart was fluttering and her breath was catching in her throat.

"Because I have never, ever loved anyone but you." He moved closer and leaned in so that his forehead was almost touching hers.

"Sebastian, I..."

Sebastian stepped back and put his finger to her lips. "Annie, you don't have to say anything. I know it's not easy. We are different people now and we live in two different places. And I think we have both been too wrapped up in trying to figure this out *right away*."

Annie shook her head and smiled. "That's exactly what I've been doing all day. Trying to figure out how I feel and what we should do..."

"Okay, then let's stop." Sebastian clapped his hands then waved them decisively. "I still have feelings for you, Annie. *Big* feelings. And I think you have feelings too...?"

"I do. Of course I do."

"Okay, then maybe for now that's all we need to know. Maybe now we should just enjoy each other's company and stop trying so hard to work out all the rest."

"That sounds like a good plan." Annie suddenly felt as if all the pressure and tension had been lifted. Suddenly, the thought of spending the next few weeks with Sebastian felt glorious and exciting instead of confusing.

"And I know how much you love planning..." Sebastian grinned. Then he tucked his hand into hers and said, "Would you care to join me for some iced tea on the terrace, Madamoiselle?"

"Absolutely," Annie replied. And as she followed him outside, she realised that she was almost – so nearly, almost – *certain*.

CHAPTER 22

ANNIE

TEN DAYS LATER

*A*nnie found Sebastian out by the empty swimming pool. He was sketching something on a large notepad.

"What's this?" she asked, sitting down beside him and crossing her legs in front of her.

"A treehouse for Mayor Debois' grandchildren. She has a very big garden, and very energetic grandchildren." Sebastian laughed and showed Annie the sketch. "I'm trying to recreate the one your grandfather made us, but I can't remember..."

"You're missing the look-out point at the top." Annie took the sketch pad from him and added a badly drawn platform and telescope above the main balcony of the treehouse.

Sebastian narrowed his eyes at it. "Wow," he said, shaking his head.

"What is it?"

"I think I have just discovered the one thing that you are truly terrible at... drawing." Sebastian looked up sheepishly then started laughing as Annie nudged him in the ribs.

"I won't argue. Art was never my strong point."

Sebastian leaned back on his elbows and looked up at the sky. His skin was shiny from the heat and as he shook his hair from his eyes he sighed and said, "They say a storm is brewing. Can you feel it?"

Annie laughed and shook her head. "Don't be ridiculous. There aren't even any clouds in the sky."

"Storms here move quickly, Annie. Can't you feel how humid it is? There's no air." Sebastian sat up again and shuffled uncomfortably.

It certainly had become more humid over the last few days. Today, particularly, was stiflingly hot. "When is this storm supposed to arrive?"

Sebastian looked at her guiltily, as if somehow he was in control of the weather. "In the next day or so."

"What about the festival? We're supposed to open on Friday. Sebastian, all our planning—"

"It'll be fine." Sebastian nudged closer and put his arm around her. "If it does come, it will be over quickly. Don't worry, okay?"

Annie leaned onto his shoulder and sighed.

"Have you heard from the hospital?"

Annie leaned away, reluctant to move from Sebastian's embrace but far too hot to be too close to another human being. "Yes, they've given her the all-clear and she'll be home tomorrow."

"That's fantastic. She has medicine for her heart?"

"Yes, but they said that will keep everything under control."

Sebastian breathed a sigh of relief and shook his head. "Ah, I'm so pleased, Annie. I was worried about her."

"I know you were." Annie reached for his hand and

squeezed it. "But, listen. To celebrate. I thought I'd make you dinner this evening..."

Sebastian frowned as if he didn't understand what she was saying. "You want to cook?"

"Well," Annie shrugged. "I don't *want* to cook. But you've played chef pretty much every night for the last fortnight, so I think it's my turn, don't you?"

Sebastian smiled, but he was looking at her strangely.

"What is it?" Annie looked over her shoulder at him as the pair of them stood up and started to walk towards the house.

"Nothing," Sebastian said quietly, still smiling. "It's just... nice."

Annie tucked her hair behind her ear. She knew what Sebastian meant; they'd spent the last ten days falling into an easy and yet still full-of-butterflies kind of rhythm where they worked on the festival for a few hours during the day and then ate and talked together until the early hours of the morning most nights. But she wanted him to say it. She wanted him to say that it was nice to be in one another's company. It was nice to have taken the pressure off and just allowed themselves to be with each other – to be themselves and to remember that, together, everything made more sense. "What's nice?" she asked coyly.

But Sebastian wasn't going to play the game. Instead, he grinned cheekily and asked, "What are you going to cook me?"

"You didn't answer my question."

"I know."

"Then I'm not answering yours, either. You'll just have to wait and see..."

139

Despite her best intentions, dinner didn't go particularly well.

"Hmm," Sebastian said, putting down his knife and fork and taking a sip of wine. "It seems we now have *two* things that you are terrible at..."

"It wasn't that bad," Annie protested, laughing at herself.

Sebastian leaned over and kissed her on the cheek. "It really was. But it's okay. I can do the cooking from now on."

That small, easy, gesture made Annie's heart flutter. But then the flutter turned to nerves. And she knew why.

Sebastian had been talking more and more about their future. Just casual comments, but comments that seemed to forget the fact that after the festival Annie should be getting on a plane and going back to England.

She kept thinking he might ask her to stay. But he hadn't. So, perhaps his references to what the future held were just accidental. Perhaps they didn't mean anything and all of this was just a bit of fun. A nice way to spend the summer.

He *still* hadn't kissed her. Not properly. And although she'd been so happy and relaxed for the past fortnight, now the festival had almost arrived, creeping thoughts of home and leaving and, *What if?* were sneaking back into her head.

She hadn't heard back from Jeremy either, and now that GiGi was coming home Annie would be forced to tell her that she'd looked at the accounts and couldn't see any way forward for the chateau... except to sell up and leave.

Without really meaning to, Annie sighed.

"Are you alright? I was only joking about the food..." Sebastian said, shuffling his chair a little closer to her.

"It's not the food. It's just..." She turned to look at him. Then shook her head at herself and said, "I'm fine. In fact, I've had an idea..."

Annie got up and trotted back into the house. She needed

Sebastian to open up about how he was feeling – about whether this was just a beautiful reminder of how they *used* to feel for one another, or whether this was something else. Something new. Something real. And she knew exactly how to start the conversation.

CHAPTER 23

SEBASTIAN

*W*atching Annie hurry inside, clearly plotting something because she had an excited glint in her eyes and the fizzing kind of aura that settled around her whenever she was hatching a plan, Sebastian breathed out slowly and tried to slow his heart rate down.

With the festival just around the corner, he suddenly felt as if time was running out.

For ten days, they had forgotten about trying to figure out what they were doing and if it would lead anywhere. They'd stopped tip-toeing around one another. They'd laughed and talked and – if he did say so himself – managed to plan the most spectacular festival for Saint-Sabran.

They worked well together. They complimented each other. Where Annie was organised and practical, Sebastian was spontaneous and creative. He brought out the best in her and she brought out the best in him.

And all of it had made him remember exactly why he had never felt for anyone the way he felt about Annie when they were teenagers.

Now, though, the pressure was beginning to build back up. And he knew she could feel it too.

The clock had begun to tick. Annie should be leaving in a few weeks. She'd had no contact with her business partner since she left and said she simply couldn't stay away much longer.

As she said it, she had looked at him as if she wanted him to say something. But he hadn't.

He wanted to. But he was torn between wanting to tell her that he couldn't bear the thought of her leaving again and wanting *her* to make the decision to stay.

When Annie returned, she was holding something. And as soon as Sebastian saw it, he knew what it was.

"Annie..." His eyes widened. "Our memory box?"

Annie grinned at him and placed it down on the table in front of them. "It was exactly where I left it. Under my old bed." She pushed it towards him and raised her eyebrows at him. "Do you want to...?"

Sebastian felt his shoulders tense a little. He knew how many love letters and postcards and photographs were in that box.

"Alright."

Slowly, Annie opened the lid and the two of them peered inside. First, she took out a stack of photographs. She handed half to Sebastian and they began to flick through.

"Oh my goodness," she said. "Look how cute we are here!" She held out a picture of the two of them when they were eleven or twelve, perched on a tree trunk down by the stream with ice cream all around their mouths. "Gramps took this one," she said with a smile.

"And this..." Sebastian laughed. "This is the one I took when you fell head-first off your bike and ended up down a ditch at the side of the road."

Annie gasped and snatched it from him. "I remember this! Instead of helping me, you took a picture!"

"You were fine." Sebastian rolled his eyes.

"You didn't know that," Annie chided.

Sebastian turned to her and ruffled her hair. "Well, I'm very sorry. Let me kiss you better now." He kissed her forehead playfully. But as he drew back, she slipped her hand into his. Instead of turning back to the photographs, she was still looking at him.

Sebastian's chest felt so tight he wasn't sure whether he was still breathing. This was the moment. She was waiting for him to kiss her, he was sure of it. But their first kiss had been so amazing, so mind-blowing... imprinted on his memory for fifteen years. What if he couldn't recreate it? What if he kissed her and she realised that all of this was...

Annie leaned in a little closer and coyly tucked her hair behind her ear. *Just do it, Sebastian,* he said to himself. *Be brave. Kiss her.*

CHAPTER 24

ANNIE

*S*ebastian was going to kiss her. Her heart was beating so fast she thought it might burst right out of her chest, and she was sure she could feel his heart doing the same.

He was so close to her... and then a loud, sharp *BUZZ* shattered their moment.

Sebastian blinked at her.

Annie took back her hand and looked towards the house. "It's the front gate. Someone's here."

Sebastian smiled reluctantly. "I'll get it. It's probably another vendor trying to secure a last-minute spot."

She almost told him not to. But he was already walking away. And when he returned, he had a strange, almost grey, expression on his face.

"Who is it, Seb?"

Sebastian glanced towards the front of the house, then looked at Annie. "It's your business partner – Jeremy."

Annie waited on the front steps. Her chest felt tight and she was jigging up and down on the balls of her feet. Sebastian was standing beside her but as Jeremy's silver rental car appeared at the end of the driveway, peeking through the slowly opening black gates, he said, "Annie, I should go."

"No," she replied, a little too quickly. "You don't have to."

Jeremy's car was approaching and Sebastian leaned down to kiss Annie on the cheek, one-two-three. "I will see you later." Then he retreated through the house.

When Jeremy got out of his car, he looked up at the sun as if it had served him a personal insult. He was wearing a suit – jacket, shirt, tie, trousers and shiny brown shoes. He must be sweltering.

Annie didn't descend the steps, just waited for him to slowly walk up to her.

"Evening," he said, tipping his head at her and making a salute-like motion.

Annie folded her arms in front of her chest. "What are you doing here, Jeremy?"

"Aren't you going to invite me inside?" Jeremy looked up at the chateau. "Impressive. Bigger than I expected."

Annie thought about making him remain on the terrace to explain himself before allowing him inside. But eventually she rolled her eyes and told him to follow her.

In the kitchen, she fetched him a tumbler of iced tea and leaned back against the counter-top, waiting for him to speak.

After sipping his tea slowly, almost enjoying keeping her in suspense, he finally said, "I got your email."

"And you couldn't have simply *replied* to it?"

"I wanted to talk to you in person – about this place, and our business." Jeremy said 'business' as if Annie had forgotten all about the agency. It made her twitch guiltily and, almost straight away, her skin started to prickle with the familiar tension she always felt back in London.

"Again, you couldn't have emailed?" Annie asked.

"I thought it would be better in person." Jeremy put down his glass and opened his hands at her, the way he always did in meetings when he was trying to convince new clients that he was trustworthy. "Listen, I know it took a lot for you to send that email. You probably left London hoping never to speak to me again, right?" He laughed a little and it made Annie's frosty exterior soften. "So, this place must mean a lot to you – for you to reach out like that."

"Yes," Annie said curtly, "it does." She paused. A flicker of hope began to dance in her belly. "So... have you found an investor? Is that why you're here?"

Jeremy shook his head and began to shrug off his suit jacket and loosen his tie. "Sadly, no."

Annie breathed in deeply through her nose and closed her eyes. Of course he hadn't. Good news would have been too much to ask.

"But I have found an alternative solution..." Jeremy smiled. It wasn't a twinkling, cheeky smile like Sebastian's; it was a self-assured, almost arrogant smile. Back in London, Annie had found it attractive. Here, it seemed utterly out of place.

"What kind of solution?" she asked tentatively.

"I have an old school friend, Charles Radcliffe. His family own a chain of luxury hotels across Europe." Jeremy waved his arms at the kitchen. "Places just like this. They're mostly in Italy right now but looking to get into France."

"Hotels?" Annie instantly hated the idea, and she knew GiGi would too.

Jeremy leaned forward and pinched an olive from the bowl on the countertop. Chewing loudly, he said, "Yes. But they're *very* sympathetically done, Annie. I can show you their portfolio. They'd treat the chateau well, and they'd give your grandmother a good price."

"She won't like it," Annie said, shaking her head.

"What other options have you got?" Jeremy asked, cocking his head to one side and chewing loudly on another olive.

Annie sighed. "Right now, none. But..."

"Listen... your grandmother is too old for a loan or investment. It's harsh but it's true. She's going to have to sell. It's the only way. *This* way... she'll get a fair deal and someone she knows will take care of the place."

"And what's in it for you?" Annie narrowed her eyes at him, speaking before she had chance to stop herself.

Jeremy chuckled. "Well, I won't lie. Charles' father has offered me a small finder's fee if I seal the deal, but I'm not trying to pull the wool over your eyes Annie – I'll give you all the facts. Let's just sit down with your grandmother and —"

"She's in hospital."

"Oh." Jeremy flinched. Family matters and anything bordering on emotional made him uncomfortable.

"She had a fall. She's fine, but they wanted to run some tests. She should be back home tomorrow."

"Great." Jeremy clapped his hands. "That's great. So, tomorrow—"

"Jeremy, listen. I appreciate you doing this... coming here." Annie was treading carefully. If the offer from Jeremy's friend really was a good one, she didn't want to chase him off. But at the same time, she wasn't going to bombard GiGi with it the second she walked in the door. "But GiGi's going to need some time to settle back in before I start talking to her about all of this."

"Alright," he said, draping his jacket over his forearm. "I'll come back tomorrow afternoon. We can talk business – because there *are* things I need your input on – and if she's up to it I'll show her Charles' portfolio. If not, I'm here for a week." He reached into his wallet and took out a business card. "I'm staying at The Grand in the next town over. I didn't think you'd want me camping out here at the chateau." He raised an eyebrow at her, then completely unexpectedly leaned forward and patted her on the shoulder. "Good to see you, Annie."

CHAPTER 25

ANNIE

*A*nnie woke feeling sick to her stomach. She should have been excited. GiGi was coming home. It was almost time for the festival. But Jeremy's arrival had changed everything.

Yesterday, she'd been excited about the festival and thinking of little more than trying to figure out what her feelings were for Sebastian. Now, she was facing the prospect of GiGi selling the chateau *and* she was no longer able to ignore the life she'd abandoned back in London.

Jeremy had made sure of that when he'd flown out to France rather than just replying to her email.

Eventually, Annie forced herself to get out of bed, open the shutters and confront the day.

The humidity was, if it was even possible, worse than yesterday. The slightest movement made her feel hot and uncomfortable and she almost couldn't bear the idea of putting clothes on.

Eventually, though, she took a freezing cold shower, put on her shorts and a loose red t-shirt, and ventured downstairs.

Sebastian was nowhere to be seen.

For the last fortnight, he'd been in the kitchen making coffee when she woke. But this morning, the chateau was empty. So, Annie brewed the coffee herself then sat on the terrace and tried to calm her nerves.

She couldn't work out whether she was nervous that GiGi would be cross she'd emailed Jeremy and invited the idea of a hotel chain buying them out. Or whether she was nervous that GiGi would *like* the idea and go for it.

Annie hated the thought of her grandmother being upset with her, but she also hated the thought of the chateau being sold to a stranger.

She sighed and scraped her hair back into a ponytail. Then she spotted Sebastian emerge from the trees.

He waved as he approached but didn't sit down beside her. Instead, he leaned back against the knee-height wall and combed his fingers through his hair.

"I thought we could go into the village for breakfast? We can check on the progress in the village square, and I will treat you to a coffee and a croissant from the bakery by the river."

Annie smiled. Whatever Sebastian thought about Jeremy's visit, he wasn't giving anything away – or behaving any differently – so she nodded enthusiastically and followed him out front.

As they drove over the bridge and pulled up beside the river, Annie smiled. The coloured flags they'd chosen had finally been strung up and were criss-crossing all the way down the street. Beyond the archway that led to the village square, she could see that the stage for the band had been erected too.

"I can't believe there are only two days to go," she said, enjoying the beat of her sandals against the shiny stone floor beneath the arch.

"It's going to be great, Annie," Sebastian put his arm around her and squeezed her shoulders. "And it looks like your grandmother will be back home to enjoy it."

Annie smiled at him, trying to force thoughts of Jeremy from her mind so that she could enjoy the moment.

After walking around the village square and ticking some things off their list, they retreated to a cafe by the river. Annie sat down and ordered coffee, while Sebastian ducked into a nearby bakery and returned with a bag full of croissants.

He handed it to her, and Annie tore it open, spreading it out on the table between them and leaning back in the chair. This was, undoubtedly, her favourite thing about being in the South of France; warm sunny mornings, people buying breakfast from bakeries and taking their food to a nearby cafe. In London, if you turned up at a coffee shop with food you'd bought elsewhere, you'd be swiftly asked to either throw it away or leave. But here, it was expected. Welcomed, even.

Sebastian didn't ask her about Jeremy. He was almost purposefully *not* asking. He simply sipped his coffee, devoured his croissant, and chatted to her about the day's final preparations.

Eventually, Annie just couldn't keep quiet any longer. "Jeremy's here because I emailed him about the chateau."

Sebastian tweaked his eyebrows upwards and swept his fingers through his hair. He let his arms relax across his chest. "You asked him to come?" There was no hint of accusation in his voice, but the question still made Annie blush.

"No. After looking at the accounts for the chateau, I just couldn't see a way out for GiGi. The only thing I could think of, apart from selling up, was trying to secure a silent investor, like the one Jeremy and I had when we started out."

"An investor?"

Annie nodded and tapped her fingers on the table. "Yes. Jeremy has contacts in the City these days, so I asked him to put some feelers out." She sighed. "But he came back blank. Apparently, with the books the way they are – and GiGi's age – investment isn't an option."

Sebastian shook his head and frowned. "Then why is Jeremy here?"

"He has a friend whose father owns a chain of luxury hotels in Europe. He said they're interested in buying the chateau. He *said* they'd be very sympathetic to the building... that they do good work."

"You don't believe him?"

Annie bit her lower lip and tried to picture Jeremy's face. "I think I do. But he's admitted he'd be given a finder's fee if it all went ahead, so I'm treading carefully."

"I can't imagine your grandmother liking the idea."

"No, I can't either."

"Are you going to tell her?"

"Not today. If she comes home, I want to get her settled in – and do some digging about this company – before I mention anything to her."

Sebastian sat up, reaching out to take Annie's hand in his as if he could sense that she was on the verge of crying even at the thought of selling the chateau. "I hate the idea too. But it might be your grandmother's only option."

Annie smiled a thin, resigned smile and tucked her hair behind her ear. It was unbearably humid today and the heat was making her neck feel sticky. "I just wish I could help. But all of my money's tied up in the business and Jeremy certainly wouldn't make it easy if I wanted to sell my shares."

Sebastian's eyes narrowed a little, as if he'd misunderstood what she'd said. "Sell your shares? You mean leave the business you and Jeremy own?"

Annie had been thinking about it for a while. The thought kept popping up in the back of her head and she was finding it increasingly hard to ignore; the longer she was in France, the more distant London felt and the harder she was finding it to imagine herself going back there.

"I thought you loved your work?" Sebastian's crystal blue eyes were searching her expression, trying to work out what she was thinking.

"I do.. I mean, I did." Annie sighed at herself. "But being here has shown me that maybe things don't have to be quite so... stressful." She laughed, as if it was a silly thing to say. "I don't know. Back home, it's like you're on a treadmill that you just can't step off of. Everything is so fast-moving and it's all about being bigger and better and more impressive than everyone else."

"And here?"

"Here..." Annie looked out at the river, at the clear blue sky and the children playing under the bridge. "It just feels different." She could feel Sebastian watching her and what she wanted to say was on the tip of her tongue. She wanted to say, *And you're here, Seb. You are here in France, and I don't know if I can leave you again.* But she didn't.

After a pause, Sebastian cleared his throat and said, "Well... I suppose we should go and visit Mayor Debois while we are here?"

"Yes," Annie said, feeling her cheeks flush as she looked at him. "I suppose we should, shouldn't we?"

CHAPTER 26

SEBASTIAN

*A*nnie said she was thinking of selling her shares. She said she was thinking of staying in France.

Sebastian had replayed the conversation in his head again and again, and he was certain that's what she'd said. But Annie had made a promise like that once before, and despite the fact he was desperate to pick her up and whirl her around and shout at the top of his voice, *Yes! Yes! Stay with me* – he didn't.

Last night, he would have. If she'd said this when they were sitting side by side looking at their memories and almost-kissing, he would have whooped and hollered and let the whole of Saint-Sabran know how overjoyed he was.

But after standing in the shade of the trees and watching Jeremy stride up the steps towards Annie, he had the sinking feeling that Annie wasn't going to cut her ties with London.

Jeremy oozed money and sophistication and glamour. His rental car probably cost more per day than Sebastian made in a week. He spoke with an upper-class lilt in his voice and would, in all likelihood, look at Sebastian as if he was a groundskeeper or handyman.

Jeremy's world was Annie's world now, and even though she said she was starting to feel like she didn't belong there, Sebastian couldn't quite believe that she'd want to leave all that behind... for him.

CHAPTER 27

ANNIE

The village was finally ready for the festival.

The mayor was thrilled, and Annie couldn't believe they had actually done it. They had ticked everything off the list and now it was just a case of setting up the tables and making sure the decorations were up.

When Annie asked about the possibility of a storm, Mayor Debois simply shrugged and said, "Whatever will be will be. Storms pass quickly here." And so they had left her to direct the set up in the village square, and gone to fetch GiGi from hospital.

As soon as they arrived back at the chateau, GiGi looked brighter and happier. As they drove up the long driveway to the house, she smiled and sighed.

"Oh, Annie, it is *good* to be home."

In the front of the car, Annie glanced at Sebastian then looked quickly away.

But, of course, GiGi spotted it.

"What is it?" she asked, instantly. "Annie? Has something happened?"

Annie was about to protest, but then she sighed and angled herself backwards so she could talk to her grandmother.

As they pulled up outside, Annie took a deep breath and said, "GiGi, I didn't want to tell you this now. I wanted you to settle in first. But..."

GiGi raised her eyebrows at Annie and waved a hand at her to hurry up.

"My business partner Jeremy is here. I emailed him and asked if he had any ideas about helping the chateau. And, well, he does have one."

GiGi's eyes brightened, but then she narrowed them and said, "I sense a 'but' coming on..."

"*But* his idea involves selling up."

GiGi breathed in the cool of the air-conditioned car and pursed her lips thoughtfully. "We already knew that was an option, Annie. I'm not sure we needed your business partner to tell us that."

"No," Annie replied. "But Jeremy has a friend whose father owns a chain of boutique hotels. He's very interested and he says it would be fair price."

GiGi blinked hard for a moment. "Boutique hotels?" She looked out of the window as she spoke, taking in the weathered exterior of the once grandiose chateau.

"Why don't we get you inside, Angelique?" Sebastian interrupted. "We can talk about this later. I'm sure you're ready for a drink and a sit down in your own chair."

GiGi smiled and reached forward to pat Sebastian's shoulder. "What I am desperate for, my boy, is to see my orchids. How are they?"

"Oh, don't worry," he replied, laughing a little. "I didn't let Annie near them."

Annie tutted at him and nudged him playfully on the

shoulder. Behind them, she noticed her grandmother give a knowing look, as if she could tell something had changed between them, but she didn't say anything.

"You're right," she said. "Let's go inside."

They had barely sat down with their iced teas, in the shade of the parasol on the terrace, when the front gate buzzed.

Once again, Sebastian answered it and returned with an almost-scowl on his face.

"Not Jeremy?" Annie asked.

Sebastian nodded.

GiGi looked at him, then at Annie. "Jeremy is your business partner?"

Annie nodded, already getting up from the table. "I'll tell him to go. It's not the right time for him to be bothering you with this, GiGi."

But GiGi shuffled in her chair and sat up a little straighter. "Annie, there's no time like the present. It's fine."

Annie wanted to protest, but before she could she heard a car door shutting and Jeremy's feet on the gravel out front. And then he was there, standing beside them in his totally out of place suit and tie.

"Angelique, it's such a pleasure to meet you. I'm very pleased you're well again." Jeremy extended his hand, but GiGi looked at it as if it might poison her.

Unsure what to do about this, Jeremy took his hand back and shoved it awkwardly into his pocket. Then, without even pausing for breath, he launched into his sales pitch.

He blathered on about the hotel chain, about his friend,

about how fabulous and sympathetic their renovations always were. And while GiGi listened, Annie's blood began to boil.

She looked up at Sebastian and saw a similarly fraught expression on his face. His hands were clenched by his sides and Annie felt as if he must have been trying *very* hard not to interrupt and ask Jeremy to leave.

Annie was about to do so herself when GiGi held up her hand to stop him from talking. "Young man," she said loudly. "Thank you. I've heard enough."

Jeremy stopped, his mouth hanging slightly open, clearly surprised at being spoken to so abruptly.

"I will accept the offer."

Jeremy paused for a moment, his expression utterly frozen, but then he grinned, clapped his hands and said, "Well, that's wonderful. I..."

GiGi shook her head. "There is no need to discuss it more now. I trust that your offer is a good one and I'll have my solicitors look it over. Thank you."

"GiGi, no." Annie whispered at first but then felt her voice clamouring at her throat and shouted, "No! You can't."

Jeremy looked at her as if she was going mad. Sebastian moved closer but didn't take her hand. And GiGi smiled softly. "Darling girl. I know this hurts. But you've seen the accounts. It's our only option, and I don't believe your friend Jeremy would have come all the way here to sell us a rotten deal. Would you?" She turned to Jeremy and stared at him, pointedly.

Unfazed, Jeremy replied, "Of course not." Then he looked at Annie. "It's a *good* deal Annie. The best you'll get. I promise you."

Suddenly, Annie couldn't look at him. Or her grandmother. Anger was bubbling up inside her and she felt like she might scream if she didn't get away from him.

"Excuse me, I'm sorry, I need a moment…" She pushed her chair back and walked past Jeremy, and Sebastian, and into the sunroom.

She kept walking through the entrance hall and out to the front steps, and then she ran.

CHAPTER 28

ANNIE

*A*nnie stopped mid-way down the driveway, panting and looking at the sky. Her heart was pounding angrily, but when she looked up it seemed to stop all together.

Above her, the sky towards the village had become so dark it was almost black.

She heard feet on the drive and turned as Sebastian jogged up behind her.

"Annie... try not to be upset. This is your grandmother's choice."

Annie shook her head at him, then pointed upwards. "Sebastian, I think they were right about the storm..."

Sebastian was standing close to her. The humidity of the air and the closeness of him was making Annie's skin hum. Above them, sky that was bright blue just a few minutes ago was now bruised with thick menacing clouds, swollen with rain, ready to erupt into a downpour at any moment.

"We should go to the village. They'll need to secure the tables they've been putting out if the wind picks up."

Despite the heat, Annie wrapped her arms around herself. "I thought you said it would pass quickly?"

"I'm sure it will. But it could still be vicious."

Annie's stomach clenched as she looked at his surly expression. "Do you think it will be?"

Sebastian released a low whistle and bit his lower lip. "I hope not. I really hope not."

By the time they arrived in the village and parked Sebastian's scooter down by the river, it seemed the entire population of Saint-Sabran was out in the square. Seeing Annie, the mayor rushed towards them, clopping over the shiny cobbled stones, waving her arms and tutting furiously. "We've done what we can to secure the tables, but it doesn't look good. We could cope with the rain, but if the wind comes too..." The mayor shook her head and squeezed Annie's hand between hers. "I think we may have to cancel the festival, Annie."

Annie swallowed hard. Ever since whisperings of the storm had begun to circulate, she'd been trying not to think the worst. But now, she didn't see how they would avoid it. All their hard work. Everything she and Sebastian had done over the last four weeks... it would be over. Just like that.

"Let's not be hasty." Sebastian was speaking calmly, looking towards the tables, which had been folded and tied together under the archways of the stone buildings surrounding the square. "It won't take long to set everything back up when the storm passes. We might have to postpone our opening night. But let's not talk of cancelling. Not yet?" He flashed his confident, cavalier smile at the mayor and she visibly blushed.

After a pause, she nodded. "Yes, I'm sure you're right. After all, Saint-Sabran has weathered many storms over the years."

"Of course it has," Annie agreed. "This will be no different." As she spoke, she tried to sound confident – like Sebastian – but before she could add that it wouldn't harm anything if they had to reschedule tomorrow's Grand Opening, it began to rain.

In the square, villagers who had been diligently tidying away anything that might blow away or be ruined by the incoming bad weather stopped in an almost comical freeze frame. Raindrops had begun to dimple the surface of the river. Annie could see them punctuating the stillness of the water. And then she began to feel them, strangely warm on her skin, but large and heavy... the kind of raindrops that were just the beginning of something much, much bigger.

The mayor glanced at Sebastian's scooter. "I don't think you two should ride back to the chateau."

Annie looked at Sebastian. "GiGi is alone..."

"Jeremy is there."

Annie raised an eyebrow at him. "Sebastian, he won't know what to do. If we go now we might make it before the rain gets worse. We need to close the shutters, secure the doors... we should have done it before we left." She could feel a familiar throb of anxiousness rising in her chest but Sebastian put his hand on her arm and caught her eyes with his.

He paused for a moment, just looking at her, then said, "Okay. We must hurry."

They had only just crossed the bridge when the angry black clouds above them opened and a tirade of rain was released. It came so quick and so heavy that Sebastian's scooter almost skidded straight off the road. Perched behind him, Annie was clinging onto his waist and trying to slow her breathing to something less panicked. Ahead, she could barely see where they were going and eventually Sebastian slowed to a stop and shouted above the rain, "Annie, we have to stop. I can't see and I feel like she's going to slip out from under me."

Annie climbed off the back of the scooter. Her hair was plastered to the side of her face and she could barely blink quickly enough to keep the water from her eyes. "We're not far... we could walk?"

Sebastian looked around them, then nodded. There was nowhere nearby to shelter and it was an equal distance between the village and the chateau, so they continued on foot.

Annie felt as if they had been walking for hours when they finally saw the black iron gates. With trembling, wet, freezing cold fingers she punched in the security code.

Nothing happened.

Sebastian tried. But, still, nothing happened. "The power must be out," he muttered. "Come..." he gestured for Annie to follow him and led her a little further along the wall. Behind a cluster of trees, part of it was crumbling and was low enough for them to climb over. Sebastian gave Annie a leg-up, then followed.

By the time the reached the chateau's front steps, the wind was blowing so hard they barely made it to the top. And when they did, the front door too refused to open.

Annie let out a frustrated cry; she was shivering and on the verge of tears. "GiGi?! Are you alright?!" She was hammering on the door, shouting at the top of her voice when she finally heard someone shout back. But it wasn't her grandmother; it was Jeremy.

"Annie! We're alright. The power is down and this fancy

door-lock system has sealed us in. Your grandmother says there should be a generator but it hasn't kicked in yet."

"Is Angelique alright?" Sebastian shouted through the door, his face etched with concern.

"Yes. She's reading in the library." There was a pause then, behind them, a bone-rattling clap of thunder shook the sky, followed almost instantly by a flash of lightening.

Behind the door, Jeremy shouted, "I'll look after her, Annie. Is there somewhere you can shelter until all this is over?"

"Yes, we'll find somewhere. Take good care of her Jeremy." Annie placed her palm on the door, but then Sebastian took her by the elbow and led her away from the front of the house.

"The stable... come."

After scurrying gingerly down the steps and around the side of the property, Annie stopped and took off her shoes. They were water logged, slippery, and slowing her down. So, she abandoned them at the edge of the lawn and followed Sebastian through the copse of trees that led to the old stable.

The door was unlocked, and Sebastian ushered her quickly inside.

Finally, they were out of the rain. For a moment, her senses struggled to readjust. Outside, they had been battered in every conceivable way. The noise and the feel and the sight of the storm had been overwhelming. Now, it was like someone had finally turned down the volume.

In the shadow of the trees, and with the pitch dark clouds overhead, the inside of Sebastian's converted stable workshop was as dark as if it were the middle of the night. Using his phone to light the room, he located some candles and started lighting them.

Annie was panting, her breath catching in her chest as she struggled to slow her heart rate. Whether it was from the effort of the journey, the fear she felt for her grandmother, or just the sheer emotional rollercoaster she'd been on the past few days – she couldn't tell. But as the old stable started to flicker into view, she began to calm down.

One half of the downstairs was now Sebastian's workshop and the other had been turned into something resembling, but not quite, a kitchen.

After lighting the candles, Sebastian brought her a towel and some dry clothes and looked sheepishly at their surroundings.

"It's not much. Not yet, but…"

Annie smiled at him. "You're very talented at what you do, aren't you?"

Sebastian rubbed the back of his neck, then as a huge clap of thunder rattled the walls and Annie winced, he said softly, "It's going to be okay. It is just… what do you British say? Just 'weather'."

Annie laughed, despite herself. "*That*," she gestured to the window, "is not *just* weather. That is like all the weather in the world, happening at once."

"We have good storms here in Provence."

"You certainly do."

"Well, seeing as we are stuck here for a while, shall we have a drink?"

"Tea?"

Sebastian chuckled. "I do have a kettle, but I was thinking…" He walked over to his make-shift kitchen and reached up onto a high shelf. "Very, very cheap but very, very nice *vin du Provence*…"

"Wine?" Annie's stomach twitched as she thought of her grandmother up at the chateau, and the village, and all of their preparations for the festival... it was hardly a time for wine.

As if he could read her mind, Sebastian nudged, "I can't think of a better time for it. To calm our nerves, no?"

His eyes twinkled in the candlelight. So, Annie nodded. "Alright." Clutching the clothes he'd offered her close to her chest, she added, "Is it okay if I change into these?"

"Ah, of course. You can go upstairs, I'll follow."

"Upstairs?" Annie looked towards the ceiling and felt her stomach tighten a little. Wasn't upstairs where his bedroom was?

"The living space is upstairs, down here is just the workroom. And a little bit of kitchen." Sebastian chuckled as he gestured to his lonely kettle, miniature fridge, and single hot-plate. Then he handed her the matches. "There are candles at the top of the stairs."

"That's very forward thinking of you." Annie wouldn't have known where to start looking for candles in her apartment back in London, let alone have some ready and at-hand in an emergency. In fact, she couldn't think of a time in recent history when she'd even used them. Mainly, she stuck to the battery-powered LED ones.

"I haven't installed electricity up there yet, so I use candles every night."

"Oh, I see." Annie felt herself start to blush but she wasn't sure why. "Alright then, I'll see you in a moment."

Sebastian nodded, then started rummaging for wine glasses in a box under the still-doorless countertop near the sink.

At the top of the stairs, just as Sebastian had promised, Annie found a cluster of candles – some large, some small. She perched on the top step and lit them, one by one, the room slowly coming to life.

Before really looking at her surroundings, desperate to get out of her wet clothes, she took the bundle Sebastian had given her into the bathroom and – by the light of her phone – changed into a pair of his joggers and a loose white T-shirt.

A few weeks ago, she would have been mortified at the thought of Sebastian seeing her like this; makeup-less, wet hair, baggy clothes that hid almost every redeeming feature she had and accentuated those she was self-conscious of. But now, she found that she didn't really mind.

Emerging from the bathroom, instead of worrying about what she looked like, she suddenly noticed what Sebastian had done with the upstairs of the chateau's old stable. And it took her breath away.

All one room, with a double bed at the end nearest the bathroom, the opposite end was finished with a wall of pure glass that wrapped round into a U-shape. With the storm raging outside, this enormous floor-to-ceiling window made Annie feel as if she was in some kind of eerie dream. But she imagined that in daylight, it would be utterly beautiful.

Just in front of the window, in true Sebastian-style, was a large indoor hammock and, beside it, a cluster of plump floor cushions. Annie picked up a couple of candles and placed them gently on a small hammered-metal coffee table that also housed a stack of French architecture magazines. Then she flopped into the centre of the cushions and felt herself let out a sigh.

Behind her, she heard footsteps on the stairs. And then, in the reflection of the glass, Sebastian appeared holding two large wine glasses.

"Do you like it?" he asked, handing her a glass and folding himself down beside her.

"Sebastian, it's beautiful. You did all of this?"

"It isn't finished." He looked down at his fingernails shyly.

169

"It's still beautiful."

Sebastian shrugged and looked up at her. "Not quite yet. But it will be. Although, I suppose now maybe it won't."

"What do you mean?" Annie's forehead wrinkled into a frown.

"Your grandmother has decided to sell. I very much doubt that whoever buys the chateau will allow me to stay."

Annie sighed and pushed her still-damp hair from her face. "I hadn't thought about that."

"I will be very sad to go. But she must do what is best for her... and for the chateau."

Annie lifted her wine glass to her lips, but couldn't bring herself to drink. Everything in her body was telling her that selling the chateau was the wrong thing. Sebastian being forced out of the beautiful home that he'd been working so hard on was wrong. Her going back to England was wrong. But she couldn't see how to make it right.

CHAPTER 29

ANNIE

*A*s the candles flickered, and the storm continued to hammer the old stable, Annie and Sebastian sipped their wine and watched the sky beyond the trees darken until it was pitch black.

"I hope Jeremy's looking after her," Annie whispered, almost to herself, picking at a small tear in the knee of the joggers she was wearing.

"He is not a nice man," Sebastian replied. "But I don't believe he is a cruel man either."

Annie nodded. "You've always been a good judge of character, haven't you?"

"I like to think so." Sebastian held her eyes as he spoke, and it made Annie feel as if she needed to look away.

Fiddling with her wine glass, she finally said what she'd been thinking of saying since they sat down: "Do you remember the last time we were stuck inside in a storm?"

For a moment, Sebastian didn't speak. And when Annie looked up, he was watching her with a strange expression on his face. "Yes. I do."

She wondered if he was remembering it too – the summer they turned sixteen, the summer they officially became girlfriend and boyfriend, before Annie broke both of their hearts and ruined it all.

Sebastian was resting his elbow on the top of his bent knee. The other leg was stretched casually over the cushions. He had changed clothes but, like Annie, his hair was still wet. He brushed it from his face and sighed, smiling at her with a smile that didn't quite reach his eyes. "We were walking by the river, the rain started and there was nowhere to shelter."

"So we climbed up into our old treehouse – the one Grandpa built us."

"And we waited there, talking about our dreams..." Sebastian's eyes were searching Annie's face. Did he just move a little closer? Or was she imagining it?

"And you asked me..." She stopped. The words trailed off and became nothing more than a small, delicate sigh that escaped her lips before she could stop it.

Sebastian put down his wine glass and, this time, Annie knew he really was leaning in closer. He reached out and took her glass, resting it beside his while not – even for a second – taking his eyes away from hers. And then, just as he had back then, he traced his index finger ever-so-gently down the side of her face. "I asked you to be my girlfriend. And you said–"

"I said..." Annie smiled at the memory, her cheeks flushing as she pictured sixteen-year-old Annie in her denim shorts, trying to play it cool. "I said, 'I'm not sure I can decide... until you kiss me.'"

Sebastian's lips curled into a grin that dimpled his cheeks. "And the kiss was what persuaded you to say yes?"

Annie tilted her head to the side and nibbled the corner of her lower lip. "Hmmm. I actually can't quite remember..."

Sebastian narrowed his eyes at her, clearly unsure of what she was about to say.

She breathed in deeply, forcing herself to be bold. "Maybe you should refresh my memory?"

Sebastian looked at her. His eyes seemed even bluer than she remembered. She wanted to lose herself in them. She wanted him to kiss her and wind back the years and pretend they hadn't spent so long apart. But just as she thought he was finally going to sweep his lips across hers – he stood up and walked over to the window.

"Sebastian?" Annie's skin felt hot and prickly, and not in a good way. Embarrassment crawled up her throat and made her voice come out as nothing more than a whisper. "I'm so sorry... I misread the situation. I thought..."

When Sebastian turned around, his usual laid back smile had vanished. He lifted both arms and put his hands behind his head, jutting out his elbows and letting out a heavy sigh. "Annie..."

Annie stood up, because it felt strange to be sitting when Sebastian looked like he was about to start pacing up and down, and waved her hands at him. "Please, it's alright. You don't have to say anything. I shouldn't have... I mean, of course you don't want to kiss me." She laughed and shook her head, looking down at her unshapely clothes. "Look at me," she shrugged, "I'm a mess. And I broke your heart. I ignored you for over a decade, and I live in London now, and–"

Sebastian stopped her by stepping forward and taking her hand in his. "Annie. Are you kidding? I *want* to kiss you. I want to kiss you more than anything in the world." He tugged playfully at the hem of her t-shirt. "Especially dressed like this." He was smiling, but then his smile wavered. "But you're right.

You did break my heart. And I'm not sure I'm brave enough to let it be broken again."

Annie felt tears welling up behind her eyes. She wanted to look away or tell him that she broke her own heart too. She wanted to tell him that she'd thought of him almost every day they'd been apart and that the moment she saw him again she knew she would fall for him all over again, but she couldn't. She just couldn't make herself say it. So, instead she pulled away from him, wrapped her arms around herself and said, "I understand."

Annie woke in Sebastian's bed. She was still wearing his scruffy joggers and his white t–shirt, and could see him asleep in the hammock. She had barely slept. The howling of the wind and the rain had kept her awake until the early hours of the morning, and she was pretty sure Sebastian had been awake too; although neither of them had spoken, she had *felt* him there.

So many times, she'd wanted to call his name so that they could lie beside one another and talk. So that she could tell him how she really felt. But she hadn't. And he hadn't either.

Beyond the window, early morning sunlight was dancing on the leaves of the trees outside. The living space Sebastian had created was nothing short of beautiful, and Annie's stomach swirled viciously as she thought of him having to leave it.

She got up and tip-toed downstairs, walking over sawdust and soft sandy wood to Sebastian's unfinished kitchen. After several attempts, she managed to fire up the hot plate and boil some water. Then she made two strong black coffees and headed back upstairs.

When she emerged, she saw that Sebastian was no longer in

the hammock – he was outside. At the far side of the room, the wrap-around floor-to-ceiling window now had a door-shaped opening and Annie noticed a balcony that she hadn't seen last night in the darkness of the storm. Sebastian was standing on it, looking out towards the village.

Annie stepped barefoot out onto the balcony and handed Sebastian a mug of coffee.

"*Merci*," he replied, immediately taking a sip despite the fact it was still far too hot.

"Did you sleep?"

Sebastian shrugged. "Ah, a little. Did you?"

"A little."

"Annie..." He wasn't looking at her. Usually he was open, friendly, totally unashamed to wear his heart on his sleeve. But this morning something was different. Annie had tried to kiss him and he had refused; *she* was the one who should be feeling awkward. And yet, Sebastian was the one behaving differently.

"Mmm?"

"Last night..."

Whatever Sebastian was about to say was drowned out by a series of shouts from just beyond the trees. "Annie?! Annie?!"

"Jeremy?" Annie looked down and squinted at the path that led from the lawn to the old stable.

Below them, Jeremy appeared. He was still wearing his suit, and when he spotted them he waved stiffly. "Are you alright?" he called.

Annie glanced at Sebastian, then back at Jeremy. "I'll be down in a second. Wait there."

When she opened the door and stepped outside, Jeremy looked her up and down – immediately noticing that she wasn't wearing her own clothes.

"Sebastian lent them to me. Mine were soaked in the storm."

"The chateau is okay, but a couple of trees seem to have come down on the driveway. Power's back though. And your grandmother is fine."

"Thank you." Annie scuffed the floor with her toe. "Thank you for looking after her."

Jeremy shrugged.

"I suppose you used the time to convince her that your friend Charles is the chateau's best hope of survival?"

"I didn't need to convince her, Annie. She'd already decided. You know that."

Annie shook her head and folded her arms in front of her chest. "This is all my fault. I should never have told you she was in trouble."

"Annie, listen. I know you think I'm the Big Bad Wolf here, but believe it or not I was trying to help you. I know I behaved like an idiot. I *am* an idiot. But I'm still your business partner and we need you back in London."

Annie couldn't help herself, she actually laughed. "Wow. Once again, Jeremy, your motives are faultless... there was me thinking you'd gone to all this trouble to help my family. Slightly misguided trouble, but still trouble. But really, you did it because *you* need me to come back to work."

Jeremy looked at her with wide eyes, as if he genuinely couldn't understand what the problem was. "Well, yes. Of course. Annie, I still care about our business – even if you seem to have forgotten about it. We set up the agency because we wanted to be important, we wanted to have our names on something fantastic, we wanted to have a luxurious lifestyle and feel proud of what we'd achieved. I still want that. And I think, deep down, you do too." Jeremy glanced over Annie's shoulder at the old stable. "All this is very lovely, for a summer vacation. But it's not *you*." He paused and caught her eyes with his. "It's not *you* Annie."

Annie felt her mouth drop open. She was speechless. She wanted to tell Jeremy how wrong he was, but a little voice in the back of her head was saying, *Is he? Is he wrong?*

Yesterday morning, she thought she wanted nothing more than to stay in France with Sebastian. She thought they could run the chateau together. She thought they could make it work. But Sebastian had rejected her. She had asked him to kiss her and he had refused. And GiGi had decided to sell the chateau. And now Annie was utterly confused.

Was Jeremy right? Was upending her life and moving to France simply a lovely idea, and an impractical reality? Like it had been when she was a teenager?

She'd backed out once before – she had returned to England, finished school, attended a great university, started a great business and created the kind of life most people would be jealous of. And she'd enjoyed it.

So, perhaps Sebastian and the chateau were meant to stay in the past? Perhaps they were nothing more than tantalising what-ifs?

She sensed movement behind her and turned to see Sebastian leaning inside the doorframe of the stable, coffee in hand, watching them. Her stomach somersaulted uneasily, as if somehow Sebastian might have been able to read her thoughts.

"We should go up to the chateau and call the mayor. Check on the village." He spoke slowly, ignoring Jeremy completely.

"Of course," Annie breathed, suddenly remembering the date. "The festival... we need to know if it can go ahead."

CHAPTER 30

SEBASTIAN

They walked up to the chateau in silence.

Sebastian hadn't slept for more than a few fitful moments all night. He just lay there, staring at the ceiling, feeling the closeness of Annie just feet away from him, and replaying the evening over, and over, and over in his mind.

He had stopped her. She had wanted to kiss him and he had pushed her away.

And now, after the way she looked at him when she brought him coffee on the balcony, he was certain he'd never get the chance again. He had blown it.

He'd been so close to a second chance with her. But he'd gotten scared. And now she was slipping away from him, and he couldn't see a way of getting her back.

CHAPTER 31

ANNIE

In her room at the top of the chateau, Annie changed out of Sebastian's clothes and back into her own. Looking out of the window, she could see the trees Jeremy had mentioned – two of them, blocking the driveway. Sebastian had tried to call the mayor, but hadn't got through. So, they'd decided there was nothing for it but to walk to the village and check what was happening.

Downstairs, Jeremy, who spoke impeccable French, was wasting no time at all in progressing with the sale of the chateau and was already on the phone to a Solicitor.

Annie paused outside the door to the study and listened for a moment. She understood only snippets of what he was saying but could see that he was enjoying himself – the scent of the commission he'd been promised spurring him on.

When Jeremy spotted her, he stepped forward and pushed the door closed. Annie sighed, then heard footsteps behind her.

"Dear girl, don't be sad."

"GiGi?"

"It's for the best." Her grandmother kissed her on both

cheeks, then clasped her hands tightly. "I am getting a good price. It's a fair deal."

"But you don't have to take it. I was trying to figure out a way..."

GiGi smiled, her eyes twinkling just a little bit less than normal. "My darling, you have looked at the accounts. If there was a way, you'd have found it by now."

Annie felt tears springing to her eyes. "But what will you do?"

"Oh, don't worry about me. I'll be fine. I expect I'll move back to Normandy, to be near my sister."

"But you don't like Elizabeth. She drives you mad."

GiGi laughed and tilted her head. "This is true. But she is family. And a change of scenery would be nice."

Annie shook her head and wiped a smudge of tears from her cheek.

"But, Annie, the real question is – what will *you* do?"

"Me?"

Her grandmother glanced towards the front terrace, where Sebastian was waiting.

Annie sighed. "Nothing. There's nothing for me to do. I'll stay and help you pack up, and then I'll go back to England."

"And what about Sebastian?"

Annie lowered her voice to a whisper. "He doesn't want me." As she said the words, her stomach twisted viciously and her throat tightened.

But her grandmother simply tutted, loudly. "Of course he wants you."

"GiGi, he doesn't. He—"

"My darling. You broke his heart when you were teenagers."

"I didn't mean to, you know that."

Annie's grandmother raised her hand to stop her talking. "Of course I do. But you can see why he would be nervous to allow it to happen again."

Annie shook her head and bit her lip.

"How can he take a chance on you again, if you haven't told him the entire truth about how you feel?"

"I..."

"Annie, think long and hard about what you want. If it's Sebastian, then tell him. It's as simple as that."

"You make it sound so easy, but how do I know if what I want is the best thing? How do I know it will work out? How do I know it won't all end in disaster?"

GiGi smiled, so wide it was almost a laugh. "You can't *know* – you can never *know* – but life is no fun if you always take the safe option. To find true happiness, you have to take a few risks."

On the way to the village, Sebastian behaved as if nothing had happened between them. He chattered away, the same as he always did. He was relaxed and smiling, like he always was. And yet, Annie could feel the whispers of unsaid feelings between them.

As they reached the outskirts of the village, however, she was finally distracted.

"Sebsatian – the river. It's..."

"Flooded."

From the top of the hill that descended into the village, they could see that the river had burst its banks. It hadn't reached the houses on the other side, but it had entirely swallowed the bridge.

"We'll have to walk around, the roads to the South might still be okay." Sebastian was about to march off along the footpath, when Annie grabbed his arm.

"Seb, look, it's the mayor."

On the opposite side of the river, Mayor Debois was standing close to the water's edge, waving at them. She was holding her cell phone and, almost instantly, Sebastian's pocket started ringing. Putting the phone on loud-speaker, he held it between himself and Annie.

"Good morning Sebastian, Annie. Are you both alright?"

"We're fine. The chateau has some trees down but nothing bad. How is the village?" Annie's muscles tensed as she waited for an answer.

"Many buildings have been damaged. Our beloved statue and part of the old church too. It will cost a fortune to repair it all, but I suppose mostly we are aright. Just a little... trapped. The river is flooded on all sides. A couple of footpaths are okay, but not enough to get vehicles in and out."

"How long will it take for the water to subside?"

"Days, maybe a week."

"A week?" Annie glanced at Sebastian. "If it was just a day or two we could postpone the festival but if it runs into next week..."

"It will clash with the big festival in Arles and we'll have no vendors." Sebastian finished her sentence for her.

"I'm sorry Annie." The mayor really did sound sorry. "I know how hard both of you worked. But I don't see—"

"Wait..." Annie spoke quietly at first, then louder. "Wait!"

Sebastian frowned at her. "Annie?"

"I have an idea. I have a brilliant idea."

Back at the chateau, Annie was pacing up and down the terrace at the back of the house with a spring in her step that she hadn't felt since her and Jeremy had first started thinking about starting the agency.

When her grandmother finally emerged from the house, Annie guided her to one of the wicker chairs and said, "GiGi, the chateau is going to have one last night of glory."

GiGi looked from Sebastian to her granddaughter. "Annie?"

"The village has been terribly damaged in the storm. The statue was knocked into by a falling tree. The church is in bad repair too. And the villagers can get in and out on foot but the bridges are flooded. "

"This is terrible..."

"Which is why we're moving the festival to the chateau."

Her grandmother frowned. Then looked at Sebastian, as if she'd somehow misunderstood Annie's English.

Sebastian raised his shoulders slowly, a hesitant smile on his lips. "It actually makes a little bit of sense when you think about it," he said.

Trying not to speak too quickly, Annie continued. "It will take a week for the water to clear, and if we delay the festival until then it will clash with Arles. But if we hold it *tomorrow night*, here at the chateau, we can turn it into a fundraiser for the village. Use the money to help do the repairs that are needed. I'm sure we won't raise a lot, but every little will help and it means that everyone who's worked so hard preparing won't be disappointed."

"Annie, that sounds wonderful but... tomorrow?" Her grandmother looked out at the lawn. "We aren't ready."

Annie sat down and took her grandmother's hands in hers. "GiGi, no one is expecting the chateau to look perfect. But in the evening, with some lights and some music... it will be beautiful."

GiGi smiled slowly and nodded. "I agree it would be a lovely way to wish our old friend farewell but, Annie, twenty-four hours to organise such an event? Can it be done?"

Annie looked at Sebastian, then back at her grandmother. "You bet it can."

CHAPTER 32

ANNIE

*A*nnie tied her hair back into a messy bun, put on her favourite blue sundress, and headed downstairs.

Unlike the night they'd gone to the festival in Mimette, Sebastian was not waiting for her at the bottom of the front steps.

Instead, she was greeted by a hubbub of people.

All around the fountain, miniature food stalls had been set up. Sebastian had hung fairy lights from the trees, lined up large upturned barrels for people to use as tables, and raided the wine cellar to set up a bar.

The mayor had helped to spread the word and, even though they weren't yet completely ready to begin, people were starting to filter up from the village.

Beside her, the blues band from Mimmette was setting up on the front terrace.

Annie smiled and thanked them in French for coming at such short notice. The saxophonist grinned. "Your French is improving, Annie," he said with a wink.

"I've been practising," she replied, smiling.

She was about to walk down and help the onion bhaji lady finish getting her stall ready, when she felt a hand on her shoulder.

"Annie..."

It was GiGi, and she was smiling proudly.

"This is absolutely beautiful. I can't think of a nicer goodbye for the chateau."

Annie sighed and shook her head. "GiGi, I..."

But her grandmother put her finger on Annie's lips and made a *shhhh* sound. "Annie, my love. Some things are not within our control."

Annie leaned closer and rested her head on her grandmother's shoulder.

"What happens to the chateau is no longer in your control." GiGi paused, then slowly said, "But some things *are* in your control."

Annie stood up straighter and tilted her head questioningly at her grandmother.

But GiGi didn't reply. She simply turned her head and looked down at the fountain, where Sebastian was standing with a hose pipe, filling it up so that he could put floating candles into it.

"He said he wanted it to be beautiful, even though it is broken," GiGi whispered.

And as Annie watched him, suddenly, she knew what she needed to do.

By nine p.m., the chateau was full of life and light and music. Annie had spent a long time watching everyone, marvelling at what she and Sebastian had created. And then she had spotted

Jeremy.

He was slinking off around the back of the house, phone in hand, taking photographs.

She caught up with him by the pool and as she tapped him on the shoulder he put his phone guiltily back into his pocket.

"Annie?" Jeremy didn't smile at her, just folded his arms in front of his chest.

"Jeremy," she released a huff of air to try and propel herself into saying what she wanted to say. "What you said yesterday morning? About this not being *me*." Annie put her hands on her hips and tried to make herself a little taller.

"Mm hmm..." Jeremy was smiling at her as if she was about to tell him he was right.

"You were wrong. So, very wrong."

Jeremy's smile faltered.

"What isn't *me* is the kind of life I was living in London. Being here the last few weeks – it's given me the time and space I needed to see that my whole life, everything I've done, it's all been because I thought it was what I *should* be doing. I've been so desperate for my parents' approval that I've put my own dreams and fantasies to one side."

"I'm sorry, Annie, but that's nonsense." Jeremy shook his head sternly. "You love the agency. You love the high-brow clients and the excitement of it all."

Annie tilted her head and smiled. In the background, she could see the silhouette of Sebastian's house in the trees. She could see the fairy lights springing to life and hear the guitar music and the chatter of the festival. "See, that's just it, Jeremy. It's crazy really that it took so long for me to figure it out. I thrive on solving problems and making things happen that people thought were impossible." She waved towards the front of the chateau. "But this is what I should be doing. Using those skills to actually make people happy. In the kind of place where I can work doing something I enjoy and have a life at the same time."

Jeremy narrowed his eyes at her, then raised his shoulders into a half-hearted shrug. "Well, that's all great. But this place isn't going to exist in a few months. So, maybe you should come back to London and forget about this floppy-haired Frenchman who's turned your head to goo and do your *real* job. The one that pays you *real* money."

As Jeremy spoke, any ounce of goodwill Annie still felt towards him evaporated into thin air. "Jeremy, that Frenchman is ten times the man you'll ever be. And, you know what? Yeah, probably my head has turned to goo. Because I've been in love with him my entire life. And being back here reminded me that I was a fool to let him go."

Jeremy blinked slowly at her, making a *scoff* sound in the back of his throat, but tugging uncomfortably at his shirt collar. "So, you're going to stay here and marry Sebastian?"

Annie swallowed hard. "I don't know what I'll do. But I do know that I'm not coming back to London."

"Fine!" Very suddenly, Jeremy's face reddened and his voice became gruff and loud. "Then my solicitor will be in touch because I didn't go into business with you wanting a silent partner, Annie. I need someone who's going to actually be *present*. So, don't think you can leave me to run things and live happily off of the proceeds because I'm telling you now – it's not happening!"

CHAPTER 33

ANNIE

*A*nnie's legs wavered as she watched Jeremy walk away from her. Her eyes were watery and the moisture was threatening to turn into full-on tears, so she shook her arms, redid her bun, and walked briskly back towards the house.

She was half-way up the steps to the terrace when she heard Sebastian's voice.

"Annie? Can I talk to you?"

"Sebastian?" Annie turned, her cheeks blushing furiously. He wanted to talk to her. But Sebastian wasn't alone; he was standing beside a smartly-dressed couple who were smiling widely at her.

Sebastian waved his hand at the woman next to him. "Annie, this is Isabelle and her fiancé Michael. They are from England."

Annie walked slowly back down the steps and extended her arm to shake hands with first Isabelle and then Michael.

Isabelle glanced at her fiancé then, still holding Annie's hand said, "We have a favour to ask you."

Slightly hesitant, and unable to distract herself from the heat of Sebastian's gaze, Annie took her hand back. "A favour?"

"We were supposed to be getting married next week in Mimette. It's been planned for months. Our families are arriving tomorrow. My dress is already here—"

Michael wrapped an arm around Isabelle's shoulders and cut in, "But our venue was damaged in the storm. They have cancelled."

"We have nowhere." Isabelle finished, widening her eyes.

Suddenly, Annie understood what was happening.

"I explained that the chateau is no longer hosting weddings," Sebastian said. "But they wanted to speak to you personally."

Annie smiled sorrowfully at the couple. "I'm sorry. Sebastian's right. We don't—"

"But what you've done here, the festival, it's so beautiful." Isabelle glanced back towards the front of the chateau where the fire pits were being lit.

Michael nodded. "We have wedding insurance, so we can pay you exactly what we'd have paid the other venue. The caterers will be happy to divert here, I'm sure. So, it'll just be..." he waved his hands, clearly not up-to-scratch with all the finer details involved with planning a wedding, "everything else."

Annie smiled as sweetly as she could. "Thank you for thinking of us, but I'm afraid we're just not wedding-ready. The chateau has been in some difficulty. We're actually selling up. I'm so sorry."

"Oh, but we wouldn't want you to change anything," Isabelle implored. "We love it exactly how it is right now. Even the fallen trees out front as benches. It's so quirky, unique..."

"People would certainly remember it," Michael added, smiling at his fiance. When he turned back to Annie, his face was more business-like. "We were paying the other venue fifteen-thousand Euro."

Annie glanced at Sebastian, swallowing hard. Fifteen-

thousand? Her brain was starting to tick with the hint of an idea. She paused, holding her breath in her lungs for longer than normal. "Could you give me a while to think about it? I'll come find you."

"Of course," Isabelle reached out and wrapped Annie into a tight embrace. "Thank you. We'll be out front."

As the couple walked away, Annie breathed out slowly and tried to order her thoughts.

"Annie... fifteen-thousand is a lot of money."

Sebastian was right. It *was* a lot of money. "But it's not enough, is it?"

Sebastian opened his mouth to speak but Annie shook her head at him. "I need some time alone, Sebastian. I need some time to think."

"Annie, wait."

She was almost back to the terrace, but Sebastian was jogging up the steps two-at-a-time and he stopped in front of her. "I think you should say 'yes' to Isabelle and Michael... if you want to."

Annie sighed. She was exhausted. "Sebastian, there's no point. Tonight was the chateau's big finale. Why prolong it?"

"Because it doesn't have to be the finale." Sebastian gestured to the wall. "Sit down with me for a moment?"

Annie did as he asked, sat down, and swung her legs gently back and forth.

"I have a solution – a way for your grandmother to keep the chateau. A way for you to stay here... if you want to." He met her eyes as he said 'if you want to' and didn't let them go.

She didn't reply.

"Annie, I heard you talking to Jeremy. I heard what you said to him."

Annie felt a warm fuzzy heat crawl up her neck towards her cheeks. Sebastian heard what she said. He heard her say she wanted to stay here. He heard her say that she'd never loved anyone the way she loved him.

Sebastian sat up a little straighter and reached for Annie's hands. His palms were warm and soft. He cleared his throat. "Annie, you remember that my parents passed away when I was very young?"

Annie frowned. "Of course. How could I forget—"

"Well, I didn't know until I was twenty-four-years-old that they left me some money. Lots of money." Sebastian paused and squeezed her hands a little tighter. "When I found out, I had no idea what to do with it. I kept a little, but the rest I wanted to be sensible with. So, I began to look for something to invest in."

Something in the back of Annie's mind started to tingle.

"I reached out to some companies who organise these things and one of them came back to me with an interesting offer. A start-up London-based business offering a very big share because they were finding it hard to secure an investment. So, they sent me the portfolio and I said *okay*."

Annie was holding her breath. Even though she thought she knew what was coming, she could still hardly believe it.

"Annie, I'm the one who invested in your company. I'm your silent investor." Sebastian's eyes were searching her face, as if he was desperately trying to figure out whether she was happy or sad or angry or ecstatic.

For a moment, she couldn't make any words come out so she just sat, staring at him.

"Annie?"

"You invested in Jeremy and I? *You* are the person we have to thank for everything that we managed to build?"

Sebastian shook his head. "You don't need to thank me."

"Seb, of course I need to thank you. You changed my life... All this time, it was you. And you never told me? You never reached out?"

"I wanted to help you, Annie. That's all."

"And you did. You did..." Annie's head was spinning. "But, what has the investment got to do with the chateau?"

"I heard what you said to Jeremy." Sebastian moved a little closer and allowed one hand to rest on Annie's knee while the other stroked her arm. It was making her feel warm and light-headed and she was struggling to focus on the relevance of his confession.

"I meant what I said..."

"I know, which is why I think we should ask Jeremy to buy our shares."

"Buy our shares? Why would he do that?"

"Because if he agrees to buy us out, we let him go ahead with the merger."

Annie let Sebastian's words sink in. "Which is what Jeremy has always wanted..."

"And if he has control of our shares..."

"He'll make far more money from the merger than he would if all three of us went through it, or if I continued refusing him."

Sebastian nodded. "Exactly."

"But, Seb, your shares will be worth so much more *after* a merger. Why would you...?" She trailed off, because she already knew why.

"Because I never did it for the money, Annie. I did it to help you. And if we sell to Jeremy, we can reinvest our money in the chateau." Sebastian waved up at the house, standing tall and proud and beautiful behind them. "This can be our fresh start. Right where we've always wanted it to be. We can work together, watch our children grow up here, become old and grey and be sickeningly happy... just as we always planned." He traced his index finger down the side of her face, then slid his hand around to the nape of her neck.

Annie shook her head and smiled at him through watery eyes. "I spent my whole life trying to forget you Sebastian – and you were right there all along."

"And while you were trying to forget me, I was waiting for you to come back. I knew you would, Annie. I knew that one day I'd be able to hold you in my arms again and tell you that I have never loved another soul. And I never will. Not if I live until I'm one-hundred years old. It will always, only, be you. And I'm so sorry I didn't tell you this the second I saw you standing there in your red dress at the airport... I should have. I should have told you weeks ago."

Annie leaned forward and pressed her forehead to Sebastian's. She reached up and stroked his stubbled jawline and let her fingers tease through his thick wavy hair. "I should have told you too," she laughed.

"I love you, Annie."

"I love you too."

And then finally, just as fireworks began to pop and fizz and explode into the sky behind the chateau, Sebastian kissed her. It was a kiss she'd been waiting over a decade to feel again... and it was even better than she remembered.

EPILOGUE

ANNIE

TWO YEARS LATER

*A*nnie stood on the balcony in front of the large glass windows of Sebastian's old stable, looking at the trees and the stream below. It had become a long-term work in progress, the rest of the chateau's renovations taking priority as its reputation, and bookings for weddings, had continued on an upward spiral.

But, despite the fact it remained unfinished, the stable was still one of Annie's favourite places. Recently, they'd decided that when it was finished – and Seb's workshop had been moved to a new location on the other side of the property – they would offer it to newlyweds who wanted to stay on for a few days in somewhere extra-special.

Annie rested her hands on her stomach. It was growing bigger by the day, and it was only just starting to dawn on her that she would be heavily pregnant at the height of both the wedding season and the French summer.

After their wedding last year, they had planned to wait a

while before starting a family; they wanted the chateau to become fully re-established before throwing a spanner in the works. But then their unexpected, but joyful, surprise came along and the decision was taken out of their hands.

On hearing the news, GiGi had announced that she would be moving to a small apartment in the village — to give them space, and to give herself a well-deserved retirement from life at the region's most popular wedding venue.

Afterwards, Annie had finally given in to Sebastian's suggestions and they had begun interviewing for a site manager, who would be in charge of all the day-to-day maintenance of the property, and an events manager, who would eventually be able to take over from Annie while she was on maternity leave... and after, too, if she decided not to return to the business full-time.

Annie was still debating whether she liked Katherine, who was fresh out of college and very keen, or Martin – older and more experienced but not quite as enthusiastic — when she heard Sebastian's scooter pull up at the chateau. Looking past the trees, she saw him wave.

As he always did, as if he couldn't wait to get to her, he jogged down the path towards the stable. But this time, he stopped down below. "Would you like to come for a swim?"

Annie smiled and sighed. A swim sounded heavenly. "Absolutely," she called back. "I'll be right down."

"Annie?" Sebastian shouted her name just as she was about to turn around.

"*Oui?*"

"*Je t'aime!*"

"I love you too, Sebastian."

THE END

Thank you for reading **Love in Provence**.

*If you love romance stories with a hint of adventure and a happy ever after, you'll love the other books in the **True Love Travels** series.*

*All books are available in Kindle Unlimited, and you can grab **Love in the Alps** totally free if you sign up to my mailing list.*

True Love Travels

Love in the Rockies

Love in Provence

Love in Tuscany

Love in The Highlands

Love at Christmas

Love in the Alps – Subscriber Exclusive – poppypennington.com

THANK YOU!

Thank you so much for reading *Love in Provence*. It's hard for me to say just how much I appreciate my readers. Especially those who get in touch. Please always feel free to email me at poppy@poppypennington.com.

If you enjoyed this book, please consider taking a moment to leave a review on Amazon. Reviews are crucial for an author's success and I would really, sincerely appreciate it.

You can leave a review at:

a amazon.com/author/poppypenningtonsmith

g goodreads.com/Poppy_Pennington_Smith

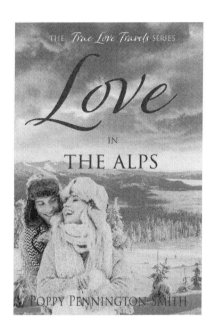

Join Poppy's mailing list to stay up to date with all of her latest releases and download the novelette *Love in the Alps* totally free!

Download Love in the Alps here:
https://BookHip.com/JCCGXV
or visit poppypennington.com

ABOUT POPPY

Poppy Pennington-Smith writes sweet, wholesome romance novels featuring tenacious women and the gorgeous guys who fall for them.

Poppy has always been a romantic at heart. A sucker for a happy ending, she loves writing books that give you a warm, fuzzy feeling.

When she's not running around after Mr. P and Mini P, Poppy can be found drinking coffee from a Frida Kahlo mug, cuddled up in a mustard yellow blanket, and watching the garden from her writing shed.

Poppy's dream-come-true is talking to readers who enjoy her books. So, please do let her know what you think of them.

You can email poppy@poppypennington.com or join the PoppyPennReaders group on Facebook to get in touch.

You can also visit www.poppypennington.com.

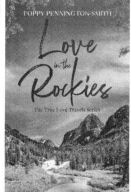

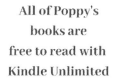

Printed in Great Britain
by Amazon